"Katy needs to be **Cruises as possible** his jaw.

"I mean, would you just walk away once she was placed with someone else?" Malory asked.

He sucked in a deep breath, then slowly let it out. "Emotionally, I'd have to, but I'd still keep an eye on her... make sure she stayed hidden."

She nodded. He'd made his decision before she'd ever arrived, and she wasn't about to change his mind.

His dark eyes moved back up to meet hers, and for the first time his guard was dropped. This wasn't the sheriff looking down at her, this was the man— strong, solid, uncertain. She had to stop herself from stepping closer still.

"I should, um—" She blushed. What she wanted right now was to slip into those muscular arms and rest her cheek against his chest. She wanted to tell him that everything would be okay because she could help him, and he wouldn't be facing this alone.

But that wasn't true, and this was dangerous territory.

SAFE IN THE
LAWMAN'S ARMS

BY
PATRICIA JOHNS

First Published in Great Britain 2016
By Mills & Boon, an imprint of HarperCollins*Publishers*
1 London Bridge Street, London, SE1 9GF

© 2016 Patty Froese Ntihemuka

ISBN: 978-0-263-91965-3

23-0216

Our policy is to use papers that are natural, renewable and recyclable products and made from wood grown in sustainable forests.The logging and manufacturing processes conform to the legal environmental regulations of the country of origin.

Printed and bound in Spain
by CPI, Barcelona

Patricia Johns writes from northern Alberta, where she lives with her husband and son. The winters are long, cold and perfectly suited to novel writing. She has a BA in English Lit, and you can find her books in Mills & Boon's Love Inspired and Mills & Boon Cherish lines.

To my husband, who inspires my romantic side.
After ten years of marriage, he still makes
my heart race.

Chapter One

The small girl looked up at Lieutenant Mike Cruise with unblinking blue eyes. One sticky hand clutched his badge—the gold six-pointed star that identified him as a sheriff in Hope, Montana. Her flaxen hair was still tousled from sleep, since she wouldn't let him comb it that morning, letting out a shriek as loud as a siren every time he came near her with a hairbrush.

He wasn't used to combing the silken curls of little girls. He was used to pushing himself to the brink on the weights at the gym, patrolling the streets of Hope and breaking up fights outside the local saloon. He was not used to this—a tiny person with more grit than he saw in the toughest ranch hand drinking away his paycheck.

"Katherine." Mike squatted down next to the little girl. "Can I have that, please?"

She shook her head, small pink lips pursed in disapproval.

"That isn't a toy, Katherine." He held out his hand, and the preschooler took a step back. "Please, give it to me."

Again, she shook her head, then wiped her nose down her sleeve, leaving a snail trail across her cheek.

Yuck. He still had to figure out how to get this child into a bathtub.

"Katherine…" He reached to take the badge from her and she opened her mouth, her shrill wail mingling with the sound of the doorbell. He heaved a sigh and pushed himself to his feet, forfeiting his badge for the moment.

He needed a nanny. Today.

Katherine watched him distrustfully as he turned toward the front door, then stepped over a pot, a sieve, an empty plastic juice jug and a small teddy bear—her favorite toys of the day. He could feel her gaze boring into the back of his T-shirt. Katherine hadn't warmed up to him and it had been two days already—two very long days.

Mike opened the door. A young woman stood on the stoop, her sandy blond hair pulled away from her face in a ponytail. A smattering of freckles across her nose brought out the chocolate brown of her eyes, making her look a little more girl-next-door than he'd been expecting of a nanny. She wore a loose pink tunic-style top and a pair of blue jeans.

"Hi," Mike said. "Miss Smythe?"

"Call me Malory." She shook his hand firmly. "Do you have my résumé?"

"Yes, the agency emailed it." He stepped aside and gestured her in. She paused in the doorway and looked around the sitting room in silent appraisal, her gaze falling on little Katherine. She bent down to the girl's level.

"Hello, sweetie," she said quietly. "What's your name?"

Katherine didn't answer, big blue eyes fixed on Malory's face dubiously.

"This is Katherine," Mike said. "She's three."

"Katherine," she said with a nod. "That's a very big name for a very little girl. Can I call you Katy?"

A smile flickered at the corners of the toddler's lips and she sidled closer to Malory, holding up Mike's badge. Malory's eyes widened in admiration and she let out an exaggerated gasp.

"What do you have there?" Malory asked, pointing at the badge. "Can I see it?"

Katy held out the badge and Malory took it, then looked up at Mike, one brow raised.

"Thanks," he said sheepishly, accepting the badge from her. "I've been trying to get that back all morning."

"Thank you, Katy. That was nice of you," Malory said and stood up.

He sighed. She hadn't used any special trick. The little girl already seemed to like this woman better than she liked him.

"Why don't you come through to the kitchen and I'll get you a coffee while we talk," Mike suggested, and he led the way through the living room, past the fireplace. This room used to be his sanctuary—big-screen TV, a wall of bookshelves, a comfortable leather couch with a footrest where he watched the game with friends.

Now it was covered in Katy's playthings, snacks and half-finished juice boxes. The kitchen was spacious, and so far still in one piece. He gestured to a stool at the counter and headed for the coffeemaker. Katy followed them, her gaze still locked on Malory.

"I just got custody of Katherine—" he paused, accepting the new name for the little girl "—Katy—two days ago. She's my cousin's daughter."

"What happened to your cousin?" Malory asked.

"Prison." He shot her a tight smile. Crystal had been involved in a fatal holdup and she'd been the only one they could pin to the scene, so she'd gotten twenty years without parole. "So Katy has been left to me, the only family member who is stable enough to care for a child." The old uncertainty swam through his gut and he sighed. "I'm a cop, as you probably figured out." He put his badge down on the counter with a click. "And I need a nanny for her."

"Understandable." Her tone was low and compassionate. "That's a lot of adjustment for both of you."

"Afraid so." As he put the coffee on, she pulled a sheet of stickers out of her purse and stuck one on Katy's nose. The girl giggled with delight—a sound he hadn't heard from her yet.

Katy obviously needed more than he had to offer.

"If her mom is in prison now, she may not have gotten all the care she needed," Malory said. "How is she doing socially?"

"I'm not sure," he admitted. "I don't know what normal looks like in a kid her age."

"Is she potty trained?"

Mike shrugged. "Sort of. There have been a lot of accidents. I wasn't sure how to tackle that."

She passed Katy another sticker, and the little girl held out her hands for more.

"How is she at bedtime? Is she anxious, afraid?"

"It takes her a while to settle down," he said. "I haven't really been enforcing much of a bedtime. I've only had her for a couple of days, and I've let her stay up with me until she falls asleep around ten or eleven, and then I put her to bed." He caught a look of faint disapproval crossing her face. "Not a long-term solution, I know."

"She needs routine and a proper bedtime, but I understand you've been thrown into the deep end here." She smiled sympathetically. "Preschoolers can be a handful at the best of times."

"Thanks." He was mildly relieved to be let off the hook. "Your references are excellent, but I've got to ask, what made you decide to work as a nanny?"

"I love kids." She met his gaze with a comfortable smile.

"Why a live-in position?" he countered. "According to your résumé, you worked as a preschool teacher before this. In Billings. You running away from something?"

It was the cop in him. He couldn't help it. He suspected the worst in everyone, it seemed, and this fresh-faced nanny was no exception.

Her earlier comfort evaporated and she smiled sadly. "Running? No. Walking briskly. I needed a change, and this seemed like a good way to get it." She gave him a crooked smile. "I'd give you my criminal-record check if I didn't think you'd already run one."

Mike chuckled. She had him there. He'd run a thorough check on her the minute the agency gave him a name.

"So what are you walking briskly from?" he asked.

"Oh, it sounds so trite when I say it out loud. I was in a long-term relationship, and we broke up. I needed the change of scenery."

It did sound a little trite, Mike had to admit, but it was believable.

"Mommy?" Katy said shyly, lifting a sticker up for Malory's approval.

"At this age, every woman is Mommy," Malory said, smiling apologetically. Then she bent down to inspect Katy's sticker. "It's lovely, Katy. But I'm not Mommy. I'm Nanny Mal."

"Nanny Mal." Katy's face lit up. "I have a bear."

"Will you show me?" Malory asked, and Katy ran from the room exuberantly.

"I haven't seen her so happy," Mike admitted. "She really seems to like you."

"Was she living with her mother until recently?" Malory inquired.

"Yes. But it wasn't a good situation. Her mother was in rehab for drug addiction, then relapsed and got involved a crime ring. If I'd known, I would have stepped in earlier, but my family doesn't have a lot to do with me."

"Because you're a sheriff," she concluded.

"Exactly. Social Services took Katy and brought

her to me. Her mother gave up all rights to her. Signed her away."

"That's tragic." Malory sighed. "Are you going to raise her as your own?"

The question didn't surprise Mike, but he wasn't entirely ready to answer it, either. He looked toward the preschooler running around the living room, pretending to search for the teddy bear that lay on the floor. She was sweet, but he knew that he was in over his head.

"I'm not planning on it," he said quietly. "But while she's with me, I'm going to need a hand."

Malory didn't answer, and when he glanced back at her, he found her gaze fixed on his face, her expression conflicted.

"You don't like that," he concluded.

"I'm not judging," she said with a shake of her head. "I think you're making the best decision you can."

Mike shrugged. He wished he were equally convinced. He refused to let the girl go into the child welfare system, but he did hope that a family—far away from Katy's own dogged beginnings—might want to adopt her.

"Well, I can pay what you've asked," he said, his tone turning professional. "Katy seems to really like you. Is there anything else I should know?" He fixed her with an appraising stare.

"No, you have all the pertinent information."

He paused for a moment, sorting through his impressions of her. She had more to her story, he could tell, but she came up clean in background check. Except for running a stop sign a few years ago, that was, but he could probably forgive her if that was the worst of her vices.

"When can you start?" he asked.

"Tomorrow."

"Great. You're hired."

A smile split her face, sparkling through her brown eyes. She was prettier than he'd been hoping for in a nanny. Too pretty to make this entirely comfortable. With a nod, he poured a cup of the promised coffee and slid it to her across the counter.

"Here you go," he said. "Your room will be upstairs next to Katy's bedroom. I hope that will be okay."

"It'll be great. Thank you very much, Sheriff—"

"Call me Mike."

"Mike." She shook his hand, and her soft fingers lingered in his grip. Then she pulled free and picked up her mug. "If it's okay, I'll get moved in today."

SUNLIGHT SPILLED THROUGH the windowpane, pooling on the hardwood floor. Malory looked around the little bedroom. A handmade quilt covered a single bed. It looked like a rag quilt, composed of different fabrics with no apparent pattern, but it was cozy nonetheless. A whitewashed wooden wardrobe stood in one corner, a wicker chair angled next to it with a pile of fresh towels on the seat. A full-length mirror hung on one wall, and a twisted rag rug lay next to the bed, completing the homey decor.

The bedroom was on the second floor of the rambling old house. This property was large and rural, so the neighbors were out of sight. It was peaceful, and she paused to listen to a bird twittering happily outside the window that overlooked the spacious backyard. Two large trees provided shade, and an overrun flower garden lined one side of a low white picket fence.

The whole scene was almost impossibly perfect, Malory thought. It reminded her of the house she used to dream about when she was a little girl, sitting alone in the small apartment after school while she waited for her mother to finish work. She used to imagine the perfect home—bright, airy, cozy, well loved. In winter, she'd picture the fireplace, roaring with heat. In the summer, she'd daydream about the backyard, dappled in sunlight.

Malory unzipped her suitcase, pulling her mind back to the present. She had a job to do.

"Nanny Mal?"

She turned to see Katy in the doorway, her worn bear clutched in her grasp and a sieve planted on her head like a little army helmet.

"Hi, sweetie." She couldn't help but chuckle at the solemn expression. "How are you doing?"

"I'm good."

"My room is right next to yours," Malory said. "And if you ever need me in the night, you can come right in, okay?"

Katy nodded, then crept closer to the suitcase and peered inside. Malory pulled out some clothes and brought them to the wardrobe.

"What's this?" Katy asked, holding up a bottle of

prenatal vitamins. Malory winced. Leave it to a toddler to zero in on the most personal, well-hidden items first.

"Those are just medicine I take to keep me healthy."

"Oh."

"And what's this?" Katy reached into the suitcase and pulled out an envelope.

"That's—" Malory sighed and took the envelope from Katy's fingers. "Never mind. It's boring grown-up stuff. Here—" Malory pulled a coloring book out of her things and passed it to her little charge. "I brought you something. Do you want to look at the pictures?"

Katy happily sat down to peruse the coloring book, and Malory opened the envelope and peeked inside at the sonogram. It was from her first ultrasound a few months earlier and it showed something the shape of a bean. But that little bean was her baby. She put a hand over her belly, feeling the soft tickle of her baby's movement. At a little over four months along, she'd started feeling it only recently.

She'd expected to look a lot more pregnant than she already did, but she could still hide her condition quite successfully with the right clothes. She appeared plumper than usual, and her waist was definitely bigger, but she didn't have that revealing baby bump yet. When was that supposed to happen? She had no idea. Regardless, her new boss hadn't noticed her pregnancy, and she was relieved for that small mercy. She needed this job, and she knew what would happen if she announced her condition at the outset—the same thing that happened to other pregnant nannies. She'd end up jobless. While she knew that she'd have to go back to live with her mother when the baby was due, she was hoping to put that off as long as possible.

"Would you like some crayons?" Malory scooped up a box of them from the bottom of her suitcase and passed them to Katy, who beamed with delight.

"The sun is green," Katy announced, pulling out a crayon and setting to work with large, jerking scribbles. "Green, green, green."

"Not yellow?" Malory asked.

"No. Green."

Malory chuckled. Well, why not? Why not have a green sun? Why couldn't Katy make her own rules?

This pregnancy hadn't been part of the plan. Malory was one of those people who planned everything. She was cautious. She was responsible. If she colored a sun, it was yellow. And then her boyfriend, Steve, told her that he didn't love her after all and took off with her best friend. Well, ex–best friend, if she was going to get technical. Two weeks later, Malory missed her period. And with everything that happened after she let Steve know... Well, she didn't want to dwell on it. Regardless, that left the financial responsibilities squarely on her own shoulders.

A tap on the door pulled her attention away from unpacking. Mike stood in the doorway. He'd changed out of his jeans and T-shirt and now stood in full uniform. A dark green button-up shirt tugged ever so slightly around his muscled biceps, paired with khaki dress pants. His heavy belt held a variety of tools, including a gun. He crossed his arms over his chest, dark eyes moving over the room, then coming back to rest on her.

"I hope I'm not in the way," he said, and she shook her head.

"Not in the least. I was just getting unpacked. Katy is coloring."

An odd look came over his face. "You're good, you know."

"I know." She laughed. "She's a sweet girl. I'm sure we'll get along very well. In fact—" Malory looked at her watch "—for her age, it's just about nap time."

"Nap time?" He frowned. "I hadn't thought of that."

"That would explain how frazzled you look." She laughed softly.

"I'm new at this," he said.

"That isn't a crime," she reassured him. "When we get a good routine going, everything will fall into place. You'll see."

She wanted to make him feel better, but she had to wonder if there would be other surprises coming. Katy might have any number of issues to deal with because of her rocky beginnings, and they'd just have to deal with them as they arose. Regardless, a well-rested child would help any situation.

He nodded, an amused smile quirking his lips. "I'm counting on that."

She reached over and brushed a curl off Katy's forehead. "Katy, come with me. It's time to lie down on your bed."

"Why?"

"We'll do this every day. We'll have a rest, and then we can play again in a little while."

"Nanny Mal?"

"Yes, sweetie?"

"Will you go away?"

Malory smiled sadly. This little girl had had too many goodbyes in her short life. "No, sweetheart. I'll be here when you wake up."

"Mommy went away."

Malory held out a hand. "I know. But I'll be here. I promise."

Katy didn't look convinced, but she consented to be led to Mike's office which had been made into her bedroom, Mike trailing behind them. She crawled up onto the bed that was squeezed in next to the desk, popping a thumb into her mouth as she lay down on the pillow. Malory eased a blanket over the tiny form, and before she could stand, Katy put out one small hand and pressed it against Malory's belly. Malory quickly moved Katy's hand away and rose to her feet, hoping that Mike hadn't noticed.

"After you rest, I have a fun game for us to play together," Malory said quickly. "But a rest first, okay?"

"But I don't want you to go." Katy's face crumpled and tears filled her eyes. "Don't go…"

Malory sighed and sank back down onto the edge of the bed. "I'll stay for a few minutes, but only if you keep your eyes closed."

Katy clamped a small hand over Malory's fingers and obediently closed her eyes. This child was desperate for some stability, and for a little while, Malory could provide it. But Katy needed more than a nanny. She needed a permanent parent. Glancing back at Mike in the doorway, she gave him a reassuring smile.

Mike stood rigidly, his face a granite mask of professional reserve. He might as well have been at a crime scene for all the emotion he allowed to slip through.

"I thought I'd get a bit of work done at the station, if you've got everything under control," he said. "Of course, I'll start paying you today—"

"We'll be fine."

He gave a curt nod, then disappeared, his footsteps echoing along the hallway and down the stairs.

Malory turned her gaze back to Katy, whose eyes were open again, staring up at her with uncertainty.

"It's okay," she said with a smile. "Close your eyes. I'm here."

A couple of minutes later, the front door opened and shut, leaving them in quiet. Her new boss interested her, and she couldn't help but wonder about the confident cop. He was handsome and intriguing—and while she tried to push that fact from her mind, she couldn't quite banish it.

Rein it in, Mal, she chided herself silently, putting a hand over the flutter in her middle. *You have someone else to worry about.*

Chapter Two

Hope, Montana, was a small ranching community consisting of a few schools, a well-stocked grocery store and a Main Street that sported murals on the sides of buildings, celebrating the Old West history. A mayor with a flair for the dramatic a few years back had dubbed the place "the Town of a Thousand Murals." There weren't exactly a thousand, but Main Street certainly did give a history lesson. The Hope Sheriff's Department was tucked between the local bank and a community hall, the side of which displayed an old-fashioned harvest with horse-drawn combines. The police station was a squat brick building, the office space cramped and out-of-date, and the parking lot only large enough to house the town's cruisers.

A warm summer breeze pushed across the plains, carrying the scent of ripening wheat from the surrounding fields. Hot prairie sunshine beat down on the dusty streets, and as Mike pulled open the police-station door, he waved to an older woman walking her dog along the sidewalk.

"Hi there," she called.

"Hi, Mrs. Hyatt," he called back, then headed in. He knew almost everyone in this town. He'd been raised in Hope and now served on the police force. That meant that most of the people he protected remembered him as a gangly kid, and he doubted that he'd ever completely grown up in their eyes. He'd matured into a muscular man, over six feet tall, but for the older ladies around town, he'd never stop being "that Cruise boy."

Mike blinked as his eyes adjusted from the afternoon sunlight. He pulled off his hat and held it under one arm as he headed inside.

"I thought you had the day off, Mike," Corporal Tuck Leavitt commented, looking up from his desk. He had a phone pinched between his cheek and his shoulder, the hold music playing loud enough for Mike to hear it clearly. Tuck had a big brush of a blond mustache and gentle, soulful eyes.

"I do." Mike tossed his hat onto his desk and sank into the creaky office chair.

"Then what are you doing here?" Tuck took a sip of coffee.

"Getting away. The nanny started today."

"Oh, yeah?" Tuck put up a finger and turned his attention to the phone as someone picked up. "Hi, this is Corporal Leavitt from the Hope Sheriff's Department..."

Mike turned away as Tuck went about verifying the alibi for a suspect. Like any other law-enforcement officer, Mike procrastinated his paperwork until either it was due to be submitted or he needed to avoid feeling something. As an escape, work always seemed better than a bar. At least he could get something productive done, and nothing was quite so numbing as filing a report in triplicate.

He turned on his computer and flipped through some forms in his inbox. But his mind kept going back to Malory. She'd been there only a few hours, but she already had Katy relaxed and happy, the chaos of the past couple of days evaporating in her calm cheerfulness. There was something about that scene—so domestic and sweet. He couldn't quite forget the solemn look on Katy's face, her hands clutching Malory's fingers as she lay on her bed.

"Thanks. I'll be in touch." Tuck hung up the phone and tossed a folder onto Mike's desk. "Alibi is rock solid."

"Figured." Mike shuffled the folder into his pile of waiting paperwork, then turned back to his computer.

"So, you hired a nanny," Tuck said with a grin. "And how is Katherine liking her?"

"She's Katy now. Malory shortened it, and Katy seemed to like it better."

"Huh. Sounds like it's going well, then."

Mike glanced up from the computer. "Can't complain."

"So what's she like?"

"Too pretty," Mike replied with a shrug. "I was hoping for a cross between Mrs. Doubtfire and Mary Poppins."

"A spoonful of sugar with masculine shoulders?" Tuck laughed.

"Too much to ask?" he said, grinning. "Instead, I

got—" He stopped, not wanting to finish his thought—he'd only sound like a lout. She really was too pretty for comfort.

"So what are you doing here at the station?" Tuck asked.

"I don't know. I feel like a third wheel back at the house. In a matter of days, my calm, relaxing home has turned into…" He shook his head, searching for the word.

"Family space? Toys everywhere, snacks, crumbs, noise."

"Yeah, pretty much." He chuckled. "At least you know what I'm talking about."

Tuck had a wife and four kids of his own.

"It's not so bad," Tuck replied. "You'll never sleep in again, or stay up late, for that matter, but it has its payoffs, too."

"This isn't long-term," Mike said. "I'll sleep in again. Don't worry about that. Anyway, Malory seems to have everything under control."

"Yeah?" Tuck didn't look convinced. "You still think you can say goodbye to that little sweetheart?"

"I'm just helping out until we can find a permanent solution," Mike replied. "I told you that before. She's better off away from the Cruise clan completely. This isn't about how cute she is. This is about what's best for her. You know what my family is like."

Tuck shrugged. "Your call, buddy."

The best decisions weren't always the easiest. Mike came from a long line of career criminals—Crystal was falling pretty close to the tree with her jail time.

For as long as Mike could remember, he'd been hearing about drug busts, arrests and attempts to escape the law—none of it from the side of the "good guys." The best thing for little Katy was to have a fresh start with a new family, far from the Cruises—as he had. He'd walked away and started a new life for himself, fighting the crime that had left indelible marks upon his childhood.

Mike pulled up his email and scanned the latest police notices. At work he felt as though he had some control—maybe not as much as he'd like, but at least he had procedures to follow. There would always be crime, and there would always be paperwork, but at least there were laws to protect the innocent.

"Speaking of your family," Tuck said. "Your dad is in town."

"What?" Mike's attention snapped back to his friend. "How do you know?"

"He started a scuffle of some sort in the Honky Tonk."

Mike sighed. That sounded about right. "Where is he now?"

Tuck shook his head. "I don't know. But I thought you might want a heads-up. He looks just the same— a bit older, maybe."

Tuck would know. He and Mike had gone to high school together and joined the sheriff's department in the same year. He was well aware of Mike's family, especially his father.

Mike didn't answer, forcing the anger back down. His father had been a real piece of work when Mike was growing up. He was a mean drunk and he was drunk a lot of the time. Mike didn't have many happy family memories after his mother died. The day his father skipped the county was a good day in his books.

"He told me to give you a message."

Mike raised his eyebrows inquiringly. "Oh?"

"He said to tell you that he's home. That's all."

"For good?" Mike frowned.

"He didn't say. I couldn't hold him. He hadn't done anything. In fact, he pulled an underage kid out of the bar when a fight broke out."

Mike sighed. He hated it when his father did something honorable. It made it harder to mentally file him away.

"He hasn't contacted you?" Tuck pressed.

"Nope. This is the first I've heard of it."

"Do you think he heard about your cousin's daughter?"

Mike shrugged. "I have no idea, but my dad hasn't had any use for me in ten years, so I highly doubt he's back for a heartwarming reunion."

Tuck shrugged. "Just passing along the message."

"Yeah. Thanks."

He pushed his rising discomfort down and focused on the paperwork in front of him. This was precisely why he was at the station—to bury himself in work. He had a feeling that whether he wanted it to or not, his life was about to tip upside down.

MALORY PUT THE LAST of the dishes into the dishwasher and closed it. Upstairs, Katy was already in bed for the night, her hair damp from her bath and her bear clutched in her arms. She'd refused to have her hair combed, and Malory hadn't pressed the point. She'd fallen asleep almost immediately after Malory kissed her good-night, the exhaustion of the past few days catching up with her.

Outside the kitchen window, the evening sunlight slanted low and golden across the backyard. The oak tree cast a long shadow, leaves rustling in the warm summer wind. This was the kind of backyard that begged for a tire swing or sandbox.

The front door opened, then banged shut again, and Malory turned to see Mike ambling into the kitchen. He held a pizza box in one hand, balanced easily on his fingertips. His broad chest tapered down to a tight waist, circled by the heavy belt of his uniform. The badge glinted against his neatly ironed shirt in the soft light of the kitchen, and Malory had to glance away, afraid to seem unprofessional admiring her boss's physique.

"I thought you might be hungry," he said, sliding the pizza onto the counter.

"Katy's already in bed," she replied. "We had some grilled cheese for supper."

"So not hungry?" He flipped open the lid to reveal a piping-hot pepperoni pie, crispy, greasy pepperoni slices buried in oozing mozzarella. She was always hungry these days, and she shot him a grin.

"Well, if you put it that way," she said. "I wouldn't turn it down."

Mike went to the cupboard and returned with two

plates. "I hope you didn't mind me going to the station today."

"That's all right."

"I thought it would be easier to have me out of the way." He smiled uncertainly and pulled a piece of pizza from the rest of the pie, strings of cheese stretching to his plate. "Dig in."

Malory followed suit, and after a big bite, she said, "I don't need you out of the way, you know."

"No? She seems happy with you."

"My job is to help with child care. I do all the things you can't do while you're working, but I shouldn't be taking over your role as her parent."

"I'm not her father. I'm her second cousin," he replied.

"And I'm not her mother. I'm paid to be here," she countered. "You're the closest thing she has to a dad right now."

His dark eyes met hers for the first time. Then his gaze flickered toward the window. "I'm afraid to let her get attached to me."

"Children need to bond to someone," she replied quietly.

"She's bonding to you."

"Yes." Malory sighed. She knew what he wanted—for her to take care of the emotional needs of the child so that when he had to let go of her, it would hurt less. She understood, even if she completely disagreed. "Kids need to know that they're loved in the world, even if they have to say goodbye. Sometimes it's good for them to see that they leave an empty space behind them and that it's hard to let go of them."

Mike didn't answer for a moment, and she wondered if she'd overstepped. Then he sighed and met her gaze.

"I'm not great with kids." His voice rumbled low. "I wouldn't even know where to start."

"You've already started." She gave him a smile. "And you're doing just fine."

He snorted and took a bite of pizza. For a few minutes they focused on eating. Malory polished off three pieces before she started to slow down. She remembered her pregnant friends saying that the baby was hungry, and it had seemed like a silly cover for eating like a teenager again. But now she understood. She was famished in a way she'd never experienced before, and it sure did feel as if the baby inside her was calling the shots.

"So, tell me about you," he said, changing the subject. "Are you from Montana?"

"No, I'm from Baltimore." She popped a stray piece of pepperoni into her mouth.

"This is a long way from home, then."

"Home is relative." She shrugged, and when he cast her a curious look, she conceded, "My mom and I moved around a lot."

"Army?" he asked.

"No, just…moving." They'd moved for so many reasons. Once to get away from a boyfriend who wouldn't accept that her mother was done with him. Several times they'd moved for promising new relationships that hadn't turned out to be as great as they'd seemed.

Malory didn't like to talk about the hard times she and her mother had had together, so she just offered a wan smile.

"That sounds kind of tough."

"It was, so I've got a soft spot for kids who need stability." She took another piece of pizza and piled the strings of cheese back on top of the slice.

"So live-in positions must be hard. Can't settle too long anywhere," he commented.

"Well, like I said, I needed the change of scenery." She shrugged. "It's not so bad. I've gotten used to it. Besides, as an adult, I have control over my life. It's an entirely different situation when you can choose to move instead of being dragged somewhere."

He didn't answer at first. His face was ruggedly handsome, his chin bristled with stubble. The lines around his dark eyes betrayed a sense of humor—the man had smiled a lot in his lifetime, even if he seemed serious now. He swallowed.

"I've lived in Hope since I was about ten," he said. "I know pretty much everyone in this town—and being a sheriff, I probably know them better than they'd like." He laughed.

"You'd think a place this small would be pretty quiet for law enforcement," she said past a bite of pizza.

He shook his head. "It's the opposite. Domestic disturbances, drunk and disorderlies, teenage house parties. It probably looks pretty quiet from the outside, but I get a bird's-eye view of pretty much everything."

She nodded. "You hold secrets."

"Enough of them. But they hold enough of mine,

too. I think that's part of what makes a place home—swapped secrets."

Malory arched a brow. "You don't seem like you'd have too many skeletons."

"Not too many personal ones," he agreed. "But my family was an out-of-control lot. When I was growing up, the cops came by my place on a weekly basis. My mom died when I was young, and my dad was all I had. He was an alcoholic, and being part of the Cruise clan wasn't a good thing, I can assure you."

"You seem to have turned out all right, though."

"I figured there had to be something more to life."

"I get that." She nodded slowly. "It wouldn't be easy, though."

"Yeah, well." He shrugged, seeming ready to drop the topic.

"So what did you do?"

"Hmm?" He wiped his lips with a napkin.

"How did you come out on top?"

"A cop took me under wing."

"Oh?"

"As a kid, I started out as a troublemaker. I got into a lot of fights. Started most of them. But one day a cruiser dropped my dad off at home—I don't remember what he'd done that time. The cop took one look at me, and he must have seen something worth saving, because he passed me his card and said I could call him if I wanted a job."

"What kind of job?" she asked.

"Yard work. He was clearing out some trees on his property. So I called him, he put me to work and he paid me. That was the first time I worked for anything, and it felt good."

She smiled. "And the rest is history?"

"Pretty much." He chuckled. "Everyone in this town knows all about my humble beginnings, so it isn't much of a secret. In fact, there are probably about six or seven old ladies quite willing to fill you in."

"Well, you're lucky," she admitted. "But you don't want to be that bighearted cop in Katy's life and help turn things around for her?"

"I might be able to do that," he agreed. "But you're forgetting that her mother is in prison. What about when she wants to meet her mom? What about when her mother wants back into her life? What about cousins and uncles and aunts who are involved in crime? I'm not her only family member, and I wouldn't be her only influence. If she stayed with me, how could I refuse to let her meet the rest of her relatives?"

Malory nodded. Much as she hated to admit it, Mike had a point. The situation was more complicated than it appeared at first glance. While Mike could easily draw some lines if he felt strongly enough, this wasn't a cut-and-dried situation, and it wasn't her decision to make.

"I think I understand," she said with a nod.

A smile twitched at the corners of his lips. "Thanks."

"But I stand by what I said—she needs to know that she matters and that when she does move on, she'll be missed. That shows her that she has value. It might not be easy on you, but it's better for her in the long run."

"I'll keep that in mind." His tone turned gruff, and

ho cleared his throat His walls had just gone back up again.

She could see a flicker of the real man underneath the tough shell, and he had a softer heart than he liked to let on.

"Thanks for the pizza," she said, licking her fingertips. "That hit the spot."

He grabbed the plates and proceeded to clean up around her. "Look, I, uh—" He glanced toward her, then turned back to the counter. "I don't normally chatter like that."

"Like what?" she asked curiously.

"Oh, family history, that kind of thing." He turned to face her, and for the first time she saw uncertainty swimming in those dark eyes. He obviously wasn't comfortable with vulnerability.

"It helps to understand the situation," she assured him. "And you can trust me to be discreet."

"Thanks."

Malory looked toward the window, where the sun was lowering temptingly in the sky. The breeze would be cool by now, and she longed for some time to herself.

"I thought I'd go for a walk," she said.

He nodded. "You can walk east, if you want to, but don't head west. There are some dogs that are pretty protective of their property out that direction."

His eyes met hers, warm and gentle, and her heart gave a lurch. If the situation were different, he'd be very easy to fall for.

She smiled. "Thanks for the warning."

Mike was afraid to get attached to Katy, and she

could understand that. She didn't really want to take a walk so much as she wanted to get out of the house. Her handsome boss was just a little too attractive, a little too intriguing… She had to say goodbye in a few months, too, and while she knew she'd miss little Katy, she had no intention of making that harder than it needed to be by getting too close to Mike, too.

If nothing else, Malory was a consummate professional.

Chapter Three

The next morning, Mike stood in the kitchen, listening to the soft peals of laughter filtering through the ceiling above. Malory was getting Katy dressed, and he had to admit that there was something very sweet about the sound of a woman's voice in the house.

"One...two...up we go!" Katy's laughter followed.

Mike took another sip of aromatic black coffee and leaned with his backside against the counter. Tonight he'd work a late shift, so this morning was free. There'd been a time—about a week ago, to be exact—when that had meant sleeping in, watching a movie or working out at the gym. Now those things seemed out of place, somehow. Malory's words from the evening before were still echoing through his mind. He had a responsibility to Katy, whether he thought he was good for the girl or not. He might be trying to keep an emotional distance, but Katy needed more from him. He wasn't even sure he knew how to give it, but maybe he could put in some effort here.

The clatter of footsteps echoed down the staircase, and a moment later, a beaming little face appeared around the corner, blond curls in pigtails and a little pink dress ruffling out around her thin legs.

"Good morning, Katy," Mike said.

"Hi." She stared up at him, big blue eyes fixed on his face. "Do you have food?"

"Uh—" He looked over at the kitchen table, where a breakfast spread awaited. "Yes."

Katy scampered over to a kitchen chair and climbed up, grabbing for the nearest box of cereal and shaking it exuberantly. Malory calmly rescued the box before it exploded, slipping it from her charge's small fingers.

"Not like that," Malory said. "I'll pour you a bowl, okay? Sit down."

Malory shot Mike a smile as she prepared Katy's bowl of cornflakes. "How did you sleep?"

"Fine." He cleared his throat, suddenly uncomfortable with this domestic scene in the middle of his house. "And you?"

"Like a baby." She chuckled as she stretched forward to reach the pitcher.

"So I was thinking about what you said last night," Mike said.

Katy wasn't paying attention, her attention on the food in front of her. Malory glanced up, brown eyes meeting his.

"I thought I might take the two of you out for ice cream this afternoon."

"Great idea," Malory agreed. She tucked her sandy-blond hair behind one ear, exposing the creamy length of her neck. "What do you think of that, Katy? Should we go out for ice cream today?"

Katy nodded and picked up a spoon in one fist as Malory set the bowl in front of her. She dug in immediately, milk dribbling down her chin. Her excitement at the prospect of breakfast saddened him. Well-fed kids tended to be pickier eaters than Katy was, and he couldn't help but wonder how many mornings she'd had the option of breakfast in her young life.

"How are you settling in?" Mike asked as Malory sat down opposite Katy and reached for her own cereal.

"This is a beautiful home. I'm very comfortable." She poured a full bowl and added milk. "It can't be easy to share your space, though."

"Oh, I survive." A smile played on his lips. Truth be told, he was having trouble thinking about anything more than the pretty nanny in his house. He could smell the sweet scent of her shampoo in the hallway that led away from the main bathroom. The sound of her cheerful tones filtered through the house in daylight, and all last night, he'd found himself uncomfortably aware that she slept down the hall.

"I took a shower late last night," Malory said. "I was worried it might wake you. Maybe we could decide on a lights-out time so that you aren't disturbed."

Mike shook his head. "No, don't worry about that. You're no bother."

Frankly, it wasn't her problem if he couldn't get his mind off her. She was just doing her job, and he'd have to practice a little more mental self-control. She was the kind of woman who would draw his eye in a social setting with her down-home good looks. If he saw her standing by the buns at a barbecue, her hair tucked behind her ear like that, he'd find his way over and introduce himself. But this was different—this was a professional line.

"I've noticed that you don't have any photos around your home," Malory said, her brown eyes meeting his. "Why is that?"

"I've mentioned the Cruise clan, haven't I?" He gave her a wry smile.

"But what about your mom?" she asked. "Don't you have pictures of her?"

He sighed. Having a woman living in his home seemed like a great idea when he needed round-the-clock child care for Katy, but right about now it made privacy a whole lot harder. "I said that my mom died, right?"

She nodded, chewing her cereal thoughtfully.

"I'm pretty sure she did, at least. I just don't know when. She ran off and left us when I was young. I don't have many memories of her, but all of them involved yelling and anger."

"Oh…" Malory winced. "I'm really sorry."

"It's okay. I've made my peace with it."

"Haven't you searched for her?"

"I have, but I couldn't find anything. My dad told me she died, so maybe he was right. He had a pretty flexible relationship with the truth, so I didn't know." He stopped when he saw the sadness swimming through Malory's eyes. "Sorry. This is why I don't talk about these things."

"Don't you have anyone you trust?" she asked quietly.

"I trust the sheriff's department. I trust the officers I work with day in and day out. I trust myself."

She nodded slowly. "That's something." Malory passed Katy half a banana, her gaze flickering toward him, then back to her charge. "It seems a little empty in here without pictures."

"I like it this way." Irritation wormed its way up inside him. He had a painful past, and pictures only served to remind him of it. He preferred to live in the present, enjoy the security of the life he worked for.

Mike let his gaze roam around his kitchen and out into the slice of living room that was visible. He hadn't actually intended to keep his home so free of pictures. One day, he always thought he'd have wedding photos, school pictures and family portraits of his own brood. But then he'd be able to protect them. He'd be able to put up a wall between them and the extended family that used and abused with apparent abandon.

Katy dropped the last of her banana into her bowl.

"You're done?" Malory asked. "Okay. Can you wash your hands by yourself, or do you need my help?"

"I can do it!" Katy declared and clattered from the table.

"You think I'm heartless, don't you?" Mike asked when they stood alone in the kitchen.

"No." She shook her head. "I think you're scarred."

He shrugged, accepting her estimation. Maybe he was. "You do realize that as a law-enforcement officer, I can't associate with known felons, right?"

"That makes sense."

"And that includes pretty much all of my family."

"Except Katy."

"Yes, except Katy." He grabbed the boxes of cereal and brought them to the cupboard. "You can't really understand where I'm coming from unless you've experienced it."

She was silent, and he glanced over to find her brown eyes trained on him. "And you don't think that they can change?" she asked.

"Change?" He chuckled bitterly. "I've been a sheriff for ten years and I've never seen anyone change."

"You changed," she countered.

"There are a few rescues," he admitted. "I was one of them. But not many. Addiction is like that. It's a vise grip."

"I could see that."

"And the lies…the constant lying. It gets to me. You know they're lying to you and you know exactly why. Everyone has a reason to lie. In court it's called motive."

"What would they lie about?" she asked, her expression clouding. She shifted in her seat.

"Everything. Anything. Do you know what it's like to not be able to trust anything someone tells you?"

"I know what it's like to find out I've been duped," she replied with a wry smile.

He paused, wondering who'd duped her in the past, but there wasn't time to ask. Katy came back down the stairs, water saturating her dress front. She looked up at Malory with a big smile. "I'm done."

"You need a tiny bit of help." Malory chuckled.

"Come on… Let's go get you cleaned up We have to brush your teeth, too…"

Malory left the room, and Mike sighed. He was talking too much. He didn't know what it was about this lovely nanny, but he found himself opening up more than he was comfortable with—talking about all the things he normally kept sealed safely inside.

Their footsteps clomped up the stairs toward the bathroom. Mike suspected that Malory was holding something back—something that made her nervous when he talked about honesty and lies. He hadn't missed the tension in her stance when the topic came up—the sheriff in him didn't just turn off when he was off duty.

And someone had duped her… For some reason, that little nugget of information stuck.

Beauty's Ice Cream was an old-fashioned place sandwiched between a coffee shop and a fish-and-chips restaurant. Outside, in the front window, faded pictures of various ice-cream treats advertised the options. A large pink ice-cream cone stood like a sentinel next to the door. It was an old building with some peeling paint and vinyl booths that could be seen through the window. Above them, the vast expanse of prairie sky stretched over the town—watery blue scratched across with wispy clouds. A warm breeze stirred, and Malory pulled her hair away from her face.

"You ready?" Mike asked, pulling open the door and stepping back. He shot her a grin.

Katy hung back, distrust etched in her tiny features.

"Don't you want ice cream?" Malory asked.

Katy scowled in the direction of the door.

"Not going in," she declared.

"Why not?" Malory bent down and then crouched next to Katy. It was awkward, and she felt her position shift to make way for the swell of her belly. She realized with a sinking feeling that she'd have trouble standing up again on her own. Something had changed even in the past few days.

"No!" Katy said, her little voice echoing across the street. "No!"

It was a tantrum...or would be soon. Malory wasn't surprised in the least.

"Really?" Malory asked, exaggerating her surprise. "Because I sure wanted ice cream."

Katy's face screwed up into a wail before the sound even started, and then she flopped herself onto the ground and howled. Malory winced.

"Wow," Mike said.

Malory shrugged. "It happens. She's three. Expect more of this."

"Over ice cream?" Mike looked incredulous.

"Why not? She's been through a lot. She doesn't know how to make sense of it. Sometimes a little venting helps."

Katy was in full tantrum now, but she wasn't going to hurt herself. Malory tried to stand up and she suddenly knew what had changed over the past couple of days—her center of gravity. Her stomach sank. This was the last thing she'd expected, and she glanced nervously toward Mike.

"Could I get a hand?" she asked, attempting to sound as natural as possible. Mike looked back at her curiously, then down at the wailing toddler. Katy hadn't let up, but she couldn't keep going forever, either.

"You okay?" Mike held out a hand, and when she took it, he lifted her easily to her feet. She stumbled forward as she rose and landed in Mike's strong arms. He was like a tank—solid with muscle and about as immovable. Her body connected with his, and Mike froze, then looked down at her in unveiled surprise.

"Wait, you're—" He released her and stepped back, looking her up and down. Malory quickly adjusted her top and turned her attention to Katy, whose wails were now abating.

"Are we ready for ice cream, then?" Malory asked brightly. "I like vanilla ice cream. What kind do you like, sweetie?"

Katy sniffled and looked up at Malory dubiously.

"I don't know," Katy said after a moment, and she got back to her feet.

Malory glanced at Mike once more, and she found his dark eyes locked on her. He knew. He'd felt her belly when he caught her. She knew she couldn't unring that bell, but she still held on to a fragment of hope that she might be able to hide her pregnancy awhile longer.

"So…" His voice was low and calm.

She sighed, giving in to the impulse and putting a hand onto her belly. "Yes, I'm pregnant. I thought I could keep it to myself, but—" She glanced down at her stomach. She'd been growing, and even the most careful dressing couldn't fully mask it any longer. She'd wondered when she'd start to show—apparently, at four and a half months.

"Okay." He looked toward the door of the shop but didn't move. "You didn't want to mention it?"

"It's personal." She threw him a defiant look, then dropped the bravado. "Mike, I need this job. The agency won't keep me on if I can't get a position, and I need the health insurance. It costs a lot to have a baby, and if I lost my health insurance..." She didn't need to finish.

"Yeah, I could see that." He sighed. "I wish you'd said something."

The wind whisked some hair into her eyes and she pulled it back irritably. He wanted her to say something? Had he ever had to risk his ability to keep his health insurance? This pregnancy had been a shock. It wasn't as if she had a contingency plan! The father was canoodling with the one woman she'd thought she'd always be able to count on, and she had to figure this all out before the baby was born.

"So am I fired?" she asked abruptly.

His dark eyes swept over her, his emotions hidden behind that mask of his. Then he shook his head. "No. Legally, you don't need to disclose that information."

She tried to suppress the sigh of relief. "But you're still probably annoyed."

He nodded slowly, and for a brief moment disappointment cracked through his professional demeanor.

"I like honesty." His expression froze her in place for what felt like an eternal moment.

Honesty. His words stung more than any firing

would have. She'd always considered herself an honest person. She believed in honesty, too, but when things got complicated, she also had a real appreciation for privacy. She'd never imagined herself pregnant and alone. She'd always wanted to be married first. Maybe even own a home. But here she was, on the cusp of single parenthood. Did he have any idea how terrifying that was?

"Let's get some ice cream," he said after a moment and pulled open the door and held it for her, a bell tinkling overhead. The gesture was sweetly old-fashioned.

"Come on, sweetie," she said softly, taking Katy's hand in hers. "We need ice cream."

Her stomach rumbled. She needed more than comfort; she was hungry. As she approached the door to the shop, held open by the broad-shouldered sheriff, she knew beyond a shadow of a doubt that nothing would ever be the same again.

She could finally admit it. She was officially eating—and working—for two.

Chapter Four

Pregnant.

Mike eyed Malory cautiously as she stepped through into the air-conditioned ice-cream shop. Her lightly scented perfume lingered. He could see it now: the way her body swelled at her waistline, the way she moved with careful, certain steps. He was a sheriff. He was supposed to see the details, and this one had swept right by him with embarrassing ease.

The only excuse he could offer up to his tattered ego was that he'd been too focused on the rest of her. They were swimming farther and farther away from the Mrs.-Doubtfire-and-Mary-Poppins hybrid he'd been hoping for.

Katy clung to Malory's hand, dancing along happily, her tantrum already forgotten. Mike stepped inside after them and caught himself short of putting a hand on Malory's back to guide her forward. He shoved his hand in his pocket instead.

What was with him? He felt a sudden protective surge, but she was his employee, nothing more. And she'd preferred to keep this information to herself, so she obviously wasn't looked for a big, strong man to take care of her.

"Look, Mike—" Malory tipped her face up to meet his gaze, worry swimming in her eyes.

"Don't worry about it," he said. "What kind of ice cream do you want?"

She blinked, then dropped her gaze to Katy. They conversed softly, and then Malory answered, "I'd like vanilla, and Katy wants the blue one. What is that, bubble gum?"

Mike scanned the tubs of ice cream through the glass guard.

"How's it going, Mike?" Trent, the store owner, asked. He was a portly man, bald on top and gray on the sides. He wore a white apron over a Beatles T-shirt. Trent's ice cream came from milk from his own dairy farm. It was a creamy delicacy that drew people from miles around, and he'd named the shop after his favorite dairy cow.

"Not too bad. Just taking these ladies out for a treat."

Mike caught the twitch in Trent's eyebrow as his gaze flickered toward Malory and back again.

"Ah." Trent shot Mike an approving grin. "And what'll it be?"

"Three cones—vanilla, chocolate and whatever the blue one is. Maybe make the blue one a kiddie cone."

"Blue raspberry."

"Sound good, Katy?" Mike asked, looking down. "The blue one is raspberry. Is that what you want?"

"Blue!" Katy declared.

"Blue it is."

Katy squirmed away, and Malory followed, leaving Mike with Trent. He could see them in the wide mirror behind the counter, getting settled at a table by a window. Trent looked after Malory with an admiring smile.

"Girlfriend?" he asked, lowering his voice.

"No, she's the new nanny." Mike shook his head. "So don't start any rumors, my friend."

"Me?" Trent chuckled. "Well, if you want a little advice—"

"I don't." Mike gave Trent a dominant expression that told the other man to back down. "But thanks."

Trent shrugged and grabbed a cone and a scoop. "Suit yourself, Mike, but if I were ten years younger and single…" He sank the scoop into the velvety surface of the vanilla ice cream. "Actually, strike that. If I were single, period, I'd ask her out myself."

"I wouldn't say that in front of Rita," Mike teased, and Trent's rosy complexion blanched ever so slightly as he scooped.

"Never. She'd kill me." He passed the cone over the glass guard.

Mike chuckled and turned to beckon Malory over. "This is yours."

Katy came running over, and Trent prepared the blue raspberry cone. Malory smiled as she accepted the cone from Mike's hand. Her cool fingers brushed his ever so slightly and she tossed him a smile of thanks before taking her first bite. He watched for her reaction and he was rewarded with an eye roll of ecstasy.

"Oh, wow," she murmured. "This is good."

"Trent makes the best," Mike agreed, and he wasn't

quite able to dampen the swell of pride to have been able to provide it.

"And this is for you," Mike said, accepting the next cone from Trent and handing it down to Katy. Katy's eyes widened in delight, and she took the treat in both hands, then waggled her tongue into the top of it.

"Let's go sit," Malory said softly, leading Katy away again toward the table.

Trent offered Mike his cone, and Mike pulled a bill out of his pocket and slapped it on the counter.

"That little girl is quite the heart stealer," Trent said as he took the bill and made change.

Mike's gaze moved toward Katy, whose mouth was already covered with blue ice cream. He couldn't help but smile.

"Yeah, she's a cutie."

"Your life will never be the same," Trent said wistfully. "I remember when my eldest was born—"

"No, no." Mike cleared his throat and accepted the change the older man held out. "This is short-term."

"Oh?" Trent's brows raised, but he shrugged and let the topic drop. "Fair enough. Good seeing you, Mike."

"Tell Rita I say hi."

"Will do."

Mike took his own cone to the far table where Malory and Katy waited, then slid into the chair opposite Malory. He was determined that this be short-term, but he found himself wondering what it would be like to keep Katy. If he had Malory here to help out—

No. He pushed the idea firmly aside. He'd thought

this through already, and Malory was pregnant. That changed a lot of things, too. He'd been right before.

"This is really good." Malory was already down to the cone, and she reached over and turned Katy's ice cream to keep it from getting lopsided, then put it back into her hands again. "Eat fast, Katy," she warned. "Or it will melt."

Mike took a thoughtful bite of his cone, but the ice cream didn't taste as good as it usually did to him. He didn't know what his problem was. It wasn't as though he'd known Malory before, or even as though he'd had plans to make something more of their relationship. But she'd held back an important detail that, while private, certainly factored into the job. And when he'd said that he preferred honesty, that was a blunt fact. He'd been lied to enough in his life, and he respected transparency.

"Look, Mike..." Malory said quietly once Katy was happily settled with her ice cream. "I'm sorry that I didn't say anything earlier. I hope you understand. If it only affected me, I might have been more forthcoming, but I'm going to have a child to provide for."

Mike nodded. "Yeah, I get it."

Having Katy here was opening his eyes to a lot of things he'd never experienced—like the amount of worry that went into a child in his care.

"I didn't think I'd be a single mom," she admitted. "But life doesn't always go according to plan."

"You don't have any support?" he asked. "What about the father?"

"Steve offered to pay for the abortion."

Mike winced. "Ouch."

What kind of a lowlife offered an abortion? He'd smack this Steve himself, given the chance.

"I could sue him for child support, true, but—" She sighed. "I'd just as well take care of my baby on my own and not have to deal with him."

"What happened exactly?" he asked. This was moving very quickly toward the personal, and she'd already made it clear that she liked her privacy, so he added, "If you don't mind me asking."

"No, no, it's fine." She waved her hand through the air. "I was dating Steve for a couple of years. After he left me for my best friend, I found out I was pregnant. I never saw it coming—him leaving me, or the baby."

"And you still told him?" He raised an eyebrow. That showed some strength right there, to give him the information at all after he'd dumped her so unceremoniously.

"It only seemed right to let him know that he had a child on the way," she replied. "And, well, you know how he reacted. I suppose it's just as well."

"Is it?" he asked uncertainly. The thought of a man treating Malory that way boiled his blood, and he'd half hoped to see his own anger mirrored in her face, but all he saw there was resignation. Whoever this guy was, that kind of reaction to the news that he'd fathered a child was unforgivable in Mike's eyes. A man stood up and took responsibility.

"My mom was on her own raising me, and she spent my entire childhood trying to rope in a husband." She shook her head. "I swore I'd never do that. I might be a single mom, but I'm not going to make my mother's mistake and think that some guy is going to rescue me. I'll do this alone."

Alone. So she'd already decided that she didn't want a man in her life. Not that it should matter to him—

Mike nodded. "Fair enough."

"And I wanted to thank you." Her gaze met his earnestly. "You could have given me my walking papers, but you didn't."

"Well, I'm not that kind of guy," he replied. It was more than that, though. Somehow, that information had sparked a protective instinct in him, and he wouldn't have been able to fire her if he'd tried. "You're here for Katy, and she really loves you already."

Malory sucked in a breath and smiled, this time the sparkle hitting those brown eyes.

"And if you need help with anything—" Mike began.

"No." Her tone was emphatic, and he bit back the last of his offer.

"No?" With no father around and no support network, he was surprised she'd turn down an offer of help.

She shook her head. "No. I'm serious. A job is enough. I can do this just fine by myself."

Malory met his gaze evenly, her lips pressed into a thin line. She meant every word, he had no doubt.

"Okay," he said with a nod. "I won't intrude."

She smiled. "Great. I think we'll get along just fine."

Mike took another bite of his cone. She was like no other woman he'd ever come across, but if she wanted her space, he could do that.

"Uh-oh, Nanny Mal." Katy sighed, and they both looked over to find the top of her cone in her lap. She poked at the softened ice cream with one finger.

Malory took a pile of napkins and set to work cleaning up what she could. A smile turned up her lips as she looked into Katy's forlorn little face. Then her honey-eyed hair fell down across her eyes, hiding them from his view.

She was certainly more appealing than Mrs. Doubtfire, he'd give her that.

THAT EVENING, MIKE sat downstairs, his feet up, emptying his brain with some sports on TV. Upstairs, the bathwater splashed in the tub, and soft voices carried down. There was something sweet about having women in the house, and he hated to admit that he liked the changes around here—the scent of perfume in the hallway, the pile of wet towels after Katy's bath, the extra plates in the sink. It was funny how such mundane details could be comforting, too.

If the facts were different, he'd be tempted to keep this. His home would feel very empty once Katy—and therefore Malory—left, even though he was trying his best to keep his emotions back.

The phone rang and he pushed himself back up, reaching for the handset.

"Mike Cruise here."

"Hello, Mr. Cruise, this is Elizabeth Nelson from the adoption agency. How are you?"

"I'm good." He sank back into the couch and muted the TV. He'd been in contact with Ms. Nelson since the day Katy arrived, and he'd already filled out a large number of forms. "Thanks for getting back to me."

"I'd love to come by and meet Katherine, if you'd be okay with that. We can start the process of finding her a family. How does that sound to you?"

"That sounds good," he said quickly. "So how does this work, exactly?"

"Well, I come for a little home visit. Then we'll make her file available to families who are looking for children. Sometimes these things take a long time. Sometimes they're surprisingly quick. It's all about finding the right match." There was a pause. "But I have to be honest. Katherine is already three, and that will make finding a match a little more difficult. Most families are looking for infants."

"Yeah, I get that," he said.

"But that doesn't make it impossible," she hurried to add. "Your situation isn't so rare. When there are deaths in a family or incarceration, there are often small children left behind without anyone to take them in. Another loving home is the best solution for everyone."

A pang of guilt stabbed at Mike's gut. Katy did have a family member, but Mike still wasn't the best solution for the kid. "So the next step is a home visit?" he prompted.

"Yes, and I'd love to come by at your earliest convenience. I have next Tuesday afternoon open."

"That could work," Mike agreed.

"Say at one?"

"Perfect. We'll be here."

After a few more pleasantries, Mike hung up and

his gaze moved toward the ceiling. Above, the plug was pulled, and the sound of water rushed through the pipes in the walls.

He'd miss this, much as he hated to admit it. He'd miss hearing laughter and bathwater. It was a silly thing to miss, but there it was. He'd never admit it out loud to anyone.

MALORY KNELT NEXT to her small charge in the middle of the floor, summer sunlight pooling on the tiles from the open bathroom window. A warm breeze pushed into the room, fluttering the white curtains. Next to them, the water drained slowly from the tub. Malory pulled the towel off Katy's wet hair and picked up a brush.

"I don't like that." Katy shook her head adamantly and clamped her hands onto her head.

"Why not?" Malory asked, squatting down next to her. They'd encountered this before.

"It's ouchie."

"I put some special conditioner in your hair so it won't hurt," Malory said.

Katy didn't answer but appeared to be thinking it over.

"What if I promise to be very, very careful? Will you let me brush your hair then?"

Tears filled Katy's eyes and when Malory came toward her, she shied away in terror. Malory looked down at the brush, and the horrible thought struck her that someone might have used a brush to punish the tiny girl in the past.

"Okay, okay..." Malory put the brush behind her

and pushed it across the floor. "No brush. Would you let me touch your hair with my fingers?"

Katy complied to that request, and Malory detangled the toddler's hair as best she could using her fingers as combs. Whatever this child had been through, it would take a lot of love and patience to win her trust again.

"What story do you want before bed, sweetie?" Malory asked as she worked on a knot.

"I want *him* to read it."

"You mean Uncle Mike?" Malory asked.

Katy nodded.

"Well, why don't you go choose a book from my bag and then you can ask him." Malory smiled as the little girl scampered off toward Malory's bedroom. Some scuffles and thumps filtered through the wall as Malory picked up the towels and wiped up the puddles on the floor. The brush lay next to the tub, and she picked it up, sadness piercing her heart.

"What did they do to you?" she whispered, then dropped the brush into a drawer.

By the time she was finished making the bathroom presentable again, Katy stood in the doorway, a book clutched against her chest.

"Got one!" she announced.

"Okay, let's go find Uncle Mike."

She'd have to fill Mike in on these developments. Maybe he could arrange some therapy for Katy. She'd need help healing from her trauma.

Katy traipsed down the stairs dressed in a nightgown, damp at the shoulders from her wet hair. When Malory caught up in the living room, she faltered. Mike sat on the couch with his feet up, the TV on a sports channel. His T-shirt tugged at his muscled chest and arms, and from the angle where Malory stood, she could see the stubble on his chin.

"Go ahead," Malory said quietly.

Mike looked up when he heard Malory's voice, and Katy moved forward, her book held over her chest like a shield.

"Uncle Mike?" she whispered.

"Yes, Katy?" He flicked off the TV and dropped the remote. Katy crept closer until she stood right in front of him.

"Uncle Mike?" she repeated breathlessly, then thrust the book out in front of her, smacking him solidly in the kneecaps.

"Ouch." He chuckled. "Do you want me to read that to you?"

She nodded but didn't make a move.

"Do you want to come sit next to me?" he asked.

Katy considered for a moment, then lifted her arms toward him. "Up," she said.

Mike glanced up at Malory uncertainly, then gently lifted the small girl up onto his lap. She pulled her knees up and settled against him, her head tipped toward his chest. Mike's expression softened, and Malory thought she saw his eyes mist, but she couldn't be sure, because he blinked quickly, cleared his throat and opened the book.

"Okay," he said. "This book is called *Lippity Loppity the Bunny*."

"Who's that?" Katy asked, pointing at the picture.

"Um…" Mike looked closer. "My guess is Lippity Loppity."

"Okay." She put her head back against his chest and heaved a deep sigh.

"'One day, Lippity Loppity the little bunny hopped away from his cozy burrow toward the big woods,'" Mike read.

"Is Lippity Loppity a girl bunny?" Katy asked.

"I think he's a boy."

"I don't like that. Lippity Loppity is a girl."

"Oh." Mike glanced up at Malory again, humor glimmering in his eyes. "Okay. I must have gotten it wrong. Let's keep reading." He turned the page. "'Lippity Loppity's mother told him'—I mean, her—'that the woods were no place for small bunnies to go alone, but Lippity Loppity didn't listen.'"

"Where is the mommy?" Katy asked.

"I don't see her in the picture," Mike said.

"What's she like?"

Mike glanced toward Malory with alarm, and she understood his discomfort. This was difficult territory considering that Katy's mother was in prison, but she needed to believe in warmth and love, even if her life experience hadn't included the kind of stability she craved. Malory shrugged, giving him a sympathetic smile. This one was his call.

"Well, I think she would be warm and snuggly," Mike said.

"Oh." Katy considered this.

"'Inside the woods—'" Mike began.

"Does Lippity Loppity have a daddy?" Malory asked.

Mike flipped forward in the story, scanning each page. When he reached the end, he flipped back to the page they were on and shrugged. "It doesn't seem to say."

"But do you know?" she asked earnestly. "Does she have a daddy?"

"Everyone has a daddy somewhere," Mike said quietly. His gaze flickered toward Malory again, and she felt a soft flutter within. She put a hand on her belly. Mike was right. Everyone did have a daddy, even if that daddy didn't want her. How did you explain that to a child? Sadness welled up inside Malory. She knew the fatherless feeling all too well, and unfortunately, so would her baby.

"Are you my daddy, Uncle Mike?" Katy asked, big blue eyes fixed on Mike's rugged face.

"I, um—" Mike cleared his throat. "No, Katy, I'm not your daddy."

"Oh." Katy's whole frame sank down in disappointment, and while Mike read the rest of the story, her glum expression didn't change.

"'And Lippity Loppity never went near the woods again,'" Mike read. "'The end.'"

Katy didn't speak, nor did she lift her head.

"Is she sleeping?" Mike whispered.

"No." Malory slid off her seat and moved next to Mike on the couch. Katy looked up at Malory dismally.

"What's the matter, sweetie?" Malory asked quietly. Katy didn't answer and likely couldn't put her thoughts into words. She was too young to grapple with the harshness of her reality. Malory held out her arms.

"Hug?" she asked.

Katy nodded and wriggled from Mike's lap onto Malory's. Mike looked sad, and Malory wished she could hold them both and soothe away this pain.

"You know what?" Malory said quietly. "Families are all different, but what matters most is the love. And your uncle Mike loves you."

Mike didn't speak, but she could see she'd said the right thing. He reached out a tentative hand and awkwardly patted Katy's back.

"Ready for bed?" he asked gruffly.

Malory scooted to the edge of the couch but realized belatedly that she wasn't going to be able to stand up.

"I need a push," she said.

"What?"

"Give me a little shove," she said with a groan, "or I'm not going to get up."

Mike put a broad, warm palm against her back and for a moment she wished she could lean into that warmth and stay there. It had been a long time since she'd felt cared for, but she knew better than to get used to this. This was a professional arrangement, not a personal one, no matter how intimate the living arrangement happened to be.

Then Mike gave her the needed momentum, and she stood up, Katy cradled in her arms. Mike rose and followed her up the stairs. She could feel the calm solidity of him behind her as they moved up the staircase together, and he paused at Katy's bedroom door as Malory carried the girl inside.

It didn't take long for Katy to snuggle under the blanket, and Malory kissed her forehead and turned off the light. The gap in the closed bedroom curtains let in a ray of summer-evening sunlight. As Malory came out into the hallway, she found Mike looking down at her tenderly.

"You did well," Malory said. "Those questions are never easy."

"Yeah?" Mike didn't move. His warm, dark eyes passed slowly over her face, and the musky scent of his cologne seemed to tug her gently closer. He leaned against the wall, his arms crossed loosely over his chest, biceps pressing against his shirtsleeves.

"Really well," she repeated, finding her voice a little breathless. "I think she's settling in nicely."

"That's thanks to you."

"And you. You were her first choice for a story."

He dropped his gaze. "I suppose. She's sweet."

"I know she gave you a bit of a rough time when she first arrived, but that little girl loves you."

"I know she's better off somewhere else, but—"

"You keep saying that," she said.

"It's true."

Malory didn't agree. It wasn't her place to convince her employer otherwise, though. If he didn't want to be a father, what should it matter to her? But it certainly mattered to one little girl.

"Have you even thought about what it would be like to keep her?" she asked.

Mike smiled sadly. "Of course."

"And?" she prodded.

"She's adorable, and the last few days have filled this house with life." He shrugged. "But she needs to be as far from the Cruises as possible. This isn't about me."

"Don't you think that your family would look for her?" she asked. "I mean, would you just walk away once she was placed with someone else?"

He sucked in a deep breath, then slowly let it out. "Emotionally, I'd have to, but I'd still keep an eye on her…make sure she stayed hidden."

"So why not keep an eye on her here?" Malory asked.

"Because I'm the first place anyone will look."

She nodded. It was the same thing he'd been saying all along. He'd made his decision before she'd ever arrived, and she wasn't about to change his mind. Except that she did feel a difference in him. He'd softened—and he'd taken her advice about opening up to Katy.

His dark eyes moved back up to meet hers, and for the first time his guard was dropped. This wasn't the sheriff looking down at her, this was the man—strong, solid, hesitant. She had to stop herself from stepping closer still. The moment seemed to slow down as their eyes met, and she knew that she needed to be cautious.

"I should, um—" She felt heat rise in her cheeks. What she wanted right now was to slip into those strong arms and rest her cheek against his chest. She wanted to tell him that everything would be okay because she could help him and he wouldn't be facing this alone. But that wasn't true, and this was dangerous territory.

He looked ready to close the distance between them. Then he smiled ruefully. "Me, too. I have to work a night shift. So I'd better get going." He straightened, turned, then stopped and looked back at her. "I know you haven't been here long," he said, "but I don't know how I'd do this without you."

A smile twitched at the corners of her lips. "All part of the job."

"Yeah." He nodded, his gaze meeting hers once more. "And you're good at it."

Then he turned and walked away, leaving her alone in the hallway. She took a deep, steadying breath.

Forget it, Mal, she told herself firmly. *You aren't going to change him.*

Chapter Five

Being in uniform had a way of changing a man. Mike liked jeans and a T-shirt when he was kicking around home, but on the street, the pressed and starched uniform gave a little extra authority. Everyone knew that Mike Cruise was in law enforcement, but there were times that he felt like a fraud.

He knew exactly where he came from, and while his adult years had been spent serving and protecting, there was a small part of himself that would always be "that Cruise kid," poised to mess it all up.

A few days had passed since he'd taken Malory and Katy out for ice cream, and they'd settled into a comfortable routine. Too comfortable, perhaps—he wasn't supposed to be getting used to this.

Tonight, as he slid into his cruiser and turned the key, he heaved a sigh of relief. There was nowhere that he felt more himself than behind the wheel.

Tuck raised a greasy bag in one hand, then buckled his seat belt. "I got those fries you like."

"Yeah?" Mike could already smell them, and it made his stomach rumble. "So how're things at home?"

They were partners and they always talked about their personal lives. With eight solid hours in a cruiser together, you either became like brothers or hated the sight of each other.

"Shana's been bugging me to take some time off," Tuck replied, reaching forward to test the radio channel and turn the volume up. "She wants to go to Disneyland."

"Sounds like a good idea to me," Mike replied. "What's the problem?"

"Do you know how much that would cost with four kids?" Tuck stroked his mustache in a movement that had become habit over the years. "We're talking hotels, restaurants, souvenirs, flights—"

"The cost of parenthood, I guess." Mike pulled out of the station parking lot and eased down Main Street toward the bar at the far side of town. A little policing was always necessary outside the Honky Tonk after the boys had some time to get a few drinks into them.

"Oh, we'll do a vacation," Tuck replied. "But we'll have to save for it first."

Mike felt a mild pang of jealousy. His wife was a dark-haired little drill sergeant with four of the best-behaved kids in town. They said "Yes, ma'am" and "No, sir." They shook hands with adults. Mike was always amazed at those kids—Tuck and Shana had done right in that department.

"So how is Katy?" Tuck asked, the bag opening with a crinkle.

"She wanted me to read to her the other night," Mike

said. He'd been keeping quiet about that story time for the past few days, but he was ready to talk about it now.

"That's cute."

"Yeah." Mike hadn't expected to feel that rush of protectiveness when he held the little girl, but he'd wanted to wrap his arms around her and keep her safe from everything out there—all the hard stuff that he knew was coming up.

"So what story did you read?"

"A Lippity Loppity something."

"*Lippity Loppity Bunny.* That's a good one. My kids loved it at her age."

Mike chuckled and reached his hand into the bag for some fries. "She asked some hard questions."

"They do that, too. Like what?"

"Who her father was." Mike popped the fries into his mouth, then signaled for a turn down a side street.

"Ouch. What'd you say?" Tuck asked.

Mike swallowed before answering. "I don't know. Just that it wasn't me, and Malory saved the day with some nice thoughts about families and love."

"She seems like a keeper," Tuck said absently.

"Which one?" Mike joked.

"Why not both?" Tuck retorted. "You could use a female touch around your place."

Mike laughed and shook his head. "Malory's pregnant, you know."

"What?"

"I can't believe I didn't notice it." Mike slowed as they eased down the residential street. These were old houses that had been around since Mike was a boy.

He knew some of the older people who lived here, but times had changed and a lot of the places had been sold to younger families.

"How far along is she?" Tuck asked.

"I didn't ask." Mike shot his partner a questioning look. "Are you supposed to ask that?"

"Yeah, if you're in any way curious about when she's going to have the baby," came the retort.

"Well, Katy isn't going to be around that long anyway," Mike replied, but the words felt wooden in his mouth. He was getting attached, despite his best intentions to the contrary.

"So I guess you'll be taking care of a toddler and a pregnant woman." Tuck chuckled. "Crash course in family life."

"Oh no. She's pretty adamant that she doesn't need anything from me. She says she's doing this one on her own."

"Yeah, well, she'll still need things," Tuck replied. "She'll be hungry all the time. Her feet are going to kill her. Her back will get sore. She'll have trouble picking things up—"

"Already there," Mike chuckled. "With picking things up, I mean. She crouched down to talk to Katy and had trouble standing. That's when I clued in." His mind went back to the feeling of her in his arms—her soft scent so close, the gentle swell of her belly pressing against his stomach. He'd realized two things in that moment: that she was pregnant, and just how attractive he found her. He'd been angry at first—she'd hidden it from him—but even in the moment he knew he didn't have that right. He pushed the memory back.

"I love it when Shana's pregnant," Tuck said. "Makes me want to have another one."

Mike put his attention into making another turn and slowing as they passed a couple of teenagers talking under a streetlight.

"She's not going to want my help," Mike said.

Tuck didn't answer, but Mike caught his partner's knowing smile, only partially hidden by his mustache. Tuck always acted as if he had some bit of inside information—and maybe he did, having been married for the better part of a decade.

The problem was, Mike was definitely attracted to Malory. That evening, standing in the hallway and having to physically restrain himself from leaning down and kissing those lips... But attraction was only that—a physical reaction. And he knew it. He also knew better than to mess with the emotions of a pregnant woman. She needed security, not games.

"She's got a plan of her own," Mike went on. "And she needs the health insurance."

"Okay, fair enough," Tuck replied.

Mike's cell phone rang, and he pulled over to a stop under another streetlight, then took out his phone.

"Corporal Mike Cruise," he answered.

"Hi, Mike, I've got a call to forward you from a Nate Cruise. You know him?"

Mike froze. "Yeah, I know him. Patch it through."

Tuck shot him an inquiring glance, but Mike stared

straight ahead, one fist clenched over the steering wheel. A moment later, there was a soft click.

"Hello?" Mike said curtly.

"That you, Mikey?"

"It's Mike now, Dad," he snapped. "To what do I owe the pleasure?"

"Can't a father just call to say hi?"

"You doing that once every ten years now?" Mike shot back.

Silence on the other end, and for a moment Mike was tempted to hang up. Something stopped him, though—that boyish longing for a "regular dad." He hadn't heard from his father since his twenty-fifth birthday, and that call had ended up being a request for money. He'd hung up the phone and vowed to never speak to the man again, but that vow hadn't been entirely necessary, since his father hadn't attempted to contact him again. Until tonight.

Mike sighed. "So how are you doing?"

"Not bad. Not bad. Better than before, that's for sure. I wanted to—" There was a pause "I wanted to see if you were okay."

"Just fine. I'm a sheriff still." He meant it as a warning. He didn't want his father to say anything incriminating that would force him to take action. At the very least, he could be spared arresting his own father.

"Yeah, I know." His father cleared his throat. "You did good."

"Where are you?" Mike asked.

"Don't worry about that," his father replied. "I just wanted to make sure you were okay."

"Did you tick off someone nasty?" Mike asked with a sigh. "Should I be watching my back?"

"No, not like that. Just—I wasn't much of a father to you, and I always felt bad about that."

Mike's brows raised in mild surprise. Was he in Alcoholics Anonymous or something, making amends for his life of addiction?

"That's an understatement," he replied coolly.

"Well, I'm sorry."

"Yeah, okay." Mike cleared his throat. "Don't worry about it."

"Okay." Another pause. "It's good to hear your voice, son. I'll let you get back to work."

"Take care." Mike punched the hang-up button and stared down at the phone with a blank expression, his emotions a jumble. He dropped his phone onto his lap and eased the car back out into the street.

"Was that—?" Tuck asked.

"My dad."

"What did he want?" he pressed.

"Nothing." Mike gripped the steering wheel in one iron fist, the muscles in his forearm rippling.

"What do you mean, nothing?" Tuck demanded.

"Nothing." Mike leveled his partner an annoyed look. "He was calling to…to say hi, I guess. Didn't ask for a penny."

"Maybe he's changed."

"I doubt it," Mike retorted. "Cruises are known for two things—crime and stubbornness. He's probably just working his way up to it, making up an elaborate lie so I'll feel sorry for him and cough up some cash."

Tuck heaved out a sigh and nodded. "Hate to agree, but you've got a point."

Tuck's support made him feel slightly better, and he stuck his hand back into the greasy bag.

"I don't like the feeling of this," Mike admitted. "Let's patrol my street tonight, too. It'll make me feel better."

He didn't know what was nagging at the back of his brain, but he'd learned to listen to his instinct with this job. His father never made contact for nothing.

Coming up at the end of the road was the local bar, the Honky Tonk. Music poured out into the street, and a couple of young men staggered into the parking lot, weaving and tripping over their own cowboy boots. In search of their truck, no doubt, to drive it drunk straight into a semi. Mike flicked on the lights, gave the siren a little whoop and turned into the parking lot.

Work was just beginning.

THE NEXT MORNING, Malory yawned and sank into a kitchen chair while the coffeemaker gurgled away from the counter. One of the downsides of being an early riser was getting up before the coffee had even started. Cool, dew-drenched air wafted in from the open kitchen window, and she sucked in a deep breath, savoring the quiet.

The aroma of percolating coffee mingled with the sweet scent of lilacs from the bushes lining the house outside. She enjoyed these times of silence when she was left alone with her thoughts.

Planning her life had seemed simple enough a few

months ago. She and Steve had been going strong—she hadn't known about the infidelity yet—and planning for the future was as simple as tucking some money into her savings account. Now everything had changed.

Working here with Mike and Katy would be easier if it weren't for their chemistry. They were comfortable together—worked well together, even. There was attraction, yes, but it was more than that. She felt as if he needed her, even though he'd never admit it. He needed more than a nanny. He needed a woman who could show him that the world was kinder than he thought—at least, pockets of it were. He needed someone he could trust, someone he could lean on. She could see his vulnerability plainly, and that was the kind of challenge that was hard to back away from.

Or was she just falling into the same traps her mother had always fallen into, and she'd find herself heartbroken, wondering why she'd let herself love a guy against her better judgment? That was probably more realistic.

The front door opened, and she paused as footsteps moved through the living room and toward the kitchen. She turned just as Mike appeared in the doorway.

"Good morning." She smiled. "The coffee is ready. Want a cup?"

"Thanks, but I can get it. Sit down."

Malory took her mug to the table, where she added milk and sugar, her eyes following the big sheriff as he tossed his hat onto the counter and grabbed a mug. He scrubbed a hand through his short-cropped hair and stifled a yawn.

"Long night." He poured his coffee, then turned back toward the table. "Are you always up this early?"

"Generally." She stirred in the milk and sugar until her coffee was taupe.

"That's probably a good habit." He slid into a chair next to her and took a sip. "I like this time of the day. Quiet."

"Hmm." She took a slow sip.

"I had a weird night."

"Oh?" She glanced up at him. "What happened?"

"Do you remember me telling you about my dad?"

"He was an alcoholic, right?"

Mike nodded. "Yeah, that's right. The last time I heard from him was about ten years ago. He called on my birthday to ask me for money to help him pay off a gambling debt."

She winced. "Did you give it to him?"

"No. I have to be careful so that I don't even give the impression of being involved in something illegal. And with my dad, there was really no way of knowing if he was telling me the truth."

"That's hard."

"He called me last night."

"What did he want?" She put her cup down on the table and turned her attention to him. His face was lined with exhaustion.

"To say hi." She caught the guilt in his expression.

"And you feel bad because you still think he's up to something," she concluded.

"Exactly. I suppose I'll know soon enough." He was silent for a moment. Then he turned toward her, his expression hardening back into the sheriff once more. "I'm telling you this because I want you to be aware. That's all. I don't mean to scare you."

She froze. "Aware of what, exactly?"

"Someone coming to the door or following you. I'm keeping an eye on you two, so you don't need to worry too much. I took a few passes by the house last night to make sure that everything was quiet."

It did make her feel more secure to think of Mike looking out for her. He was big, broad and immovable, and she had a feeling that if anyone tried to get through him, it would be like slamming up against a boulder. But why was he so worried if his father's biggest vice was hitting up family members for money?

"Your father has some enemies?" she guessed.

"In that world, Malory, everyone has enemies." He took a sip of coffee, and his gaze moved toward the window. "It's a dark place. You don't realize how dark until you manage to crawl out."

"You mean poverty?" she asked.

"Poverty?" He shook his head. "There's no shame in being poor. No, I mean a life of crime and addiction. That's completely different."

Malory looked at him thoughtfully for a moment, then said, "And I imagine when he called last night, it brought you right back there."

"Hmm?" His dark eyes met hers, his expression unreadable. "No, I'm a grown man now, and no one gets to turn back that clock."

"Not even your father?" she asked.

Mike chuckled, the sound low and deep. "Do I look like I ever feel small and afraid?"

Malory regarded the large-shouldered man sitting next to her. His elbows rested on the table, his biceps pressing against his shirtsleeves, the mug dwarfed in his hands. His neck was thick and his chest was well muscled—nothing was small about this man.

"I'd say that appearances can be deceiving," she said at last.

"Maybe so," he agreed. "But not this time around. Just keep an eye out, and if you feel like something is off, give me a call on my cell."

She nodded. "I will."

"Good." He relaxed and leaned back in his chair. "How is Katy?"

"She's doing pretty well, considering." She paused. "Did you know that she's afraid of hairbrushes?"

"I thought she was scared of me."

"No, she's been totally panicking when I try to brush her hair. There is something about a brush." She swallowed a lump that rose in her throat. "Is it possible that she was physically abused?"

"I don't know." His voice was low. "The poor kid. My cousin was in rough shape. I have no idea who she had coming through her home or if she could have been capable of it herself." He winced. "You know, if things were different, I'd keep Katy myself. No one would ever lay a finger on her again."

Malory felt a rush of hope. "It is a possibility, you know."

"I've got to trust my instinct on this, Malory." He

sucked in a deep breath. "We have a meeting with the adoption agency tomorrow afternoon. It's just a preliminary visit for them to see Katy and gather some information."

Malory nodded, stunned, her hope instantly deflating once more. He gave her an apologetic smile.

"Okay," she said, forcing professionalism into her tone. "What should we tell Katy about it?"

His gaze met hers, and she found uncertainty in his eyes. "I was hoping you'd have an idea about that."

She thought for a moment, considering possible scenarios. What mattered here was how Katy pulled through.

"Maybe since it's a preliminary visit, we shouldn't say anything. Things might happen quickly, but they also might not. I'd hate for her to feel like she wasn't wanted if the process turned out to be slow."

"Yeah, that's a good point." He nodded. "Thanks."

"What time is the visit?"

"They'll be here at one."

"Okay." She nodded. "I'll make sure we're all presentable by then."

He looked as though he wanted to say something else, but instead, he pressed his lips together, then turned and left the room. She'd known that this was coming, but it still left her with an empty feeling in her gut. This was Mike's choice to make, but she couldn't help wishing he'd change his mind before it was too late.

Chapter Six

The next afternoon, the adoption-agency representative arrived in a small blue sedan at exactly one o'clock. She was a middle-aged woman with a short white hairdo and a maternal smile, but her sharp blue eyes didn't seem to miss anything. She stepped inside and her gaze swept around the room. She reminded him of a grade-school teacher he'd had—the kind of woman who could make an A minus feel like a failure for the kid who could do better and a C feel like his biggest success. He'd been the kid with the C.

"Good morning, Mr. Cruise." Her voice was clipped and cheerful. "I'm Elizabeth Nelson with the Longman Adoption Agency. I'm here for our preliminary meeting. Let's get right down to it, shall we?"

"Absolutely." He smiled and stepped back. "Please come in."

She took a full turn, peering around the place over her half-glasses. "Where is the little one?"

"She's with her nanny outside. I thought it might give us a chance to talk alone."

"So you've hired some additional help with child care?" she asked.

"I work full-time for the sheriff's department, so I needed someone around the clock to help with her." He didn't care to admit that even when he had taken a few days off, he'd been completely outgunned by the girl. He was used to being viewed as competent and in control, but a child changed all the rules. She had little to no respect for the badge.

Ms. Nelson nodded. "Have you told the child about the adoption?"

"No, ma'am."

He gestured her to sit on the couch, and she complied, fishing a legal pad out of her oversize purse.

"That might be for the best," she said. "I believe I mentioned the challenge of placing older children when we spoke. Infants are easy, but the placement rate goes down once the child passes the first year."

He nodded, grateful that he had Malory's advice in this. He'd been more inclined to try to explain it to Katy, and he'd likely have only made things worse. What did he know about raising a little girl?

"Now, Mr. Cruise," Ms. Nelson said, "I understand that you are Katherine's legal guardian now."

"Yes, I am." He nodded. "Her mother is in prison for another nineteen years. She gave up all legal rights to her daughter. I think it's best to give her a home as far away from her mother's family as possible."

"But, if you'll forgive me, you do seem like an excellent solution for the child. You're well respected in your community and financially able to provide—"

"And her mother's first cousin." He shook his head. "I was raised in this family, and I know what I'm talking about. She's better off with a fresh start."

"Understood." She nodded and made a note on her pad of paper.

"Are you willing to remain Katherine's guardian if an immediate placement isn't possible?"

Mike was silent for moment, considering his options. "Yes," he said finally. "I don't want her in the system."

She made another note on her pad of paper. "For how long?"

"You mean, how long am I willing to stand in?" he asked.

"Exactly."

"As long as I have to." He wasn't exactly going to throw the child out by a certain deadline.

She nodded again, made another couple of notes, then looked up with a prim smile. "Can I meet her?"

"You bet."

He stood up, suddenly realizing that adoption was a very permanent solution. The idea of finding a new home for Katy had seemed so logical and necessary at first. Giving her up wasn't going to be as easy as he'd imagined, but he pushed his discomfort down. Logic had to prevail. Katy deserved more. And there was always the chance that there wouldn't be a family looking for a child her age at this time.

Was that hope he felt welling up at that prospect?

Ambling toward the kitchen and the back door, he

said over his shoulder, "Let me just go call them in. They're having a picnic in the backyard."

MALORY AND KATY sat on a red checkered picnic blanket— something Malory had found in the top of the closet in her bedroom—with a plate of finger sandwiches and two juice boxes between them. A playful wind whispered through the trees that stretched overhead, but her mind wasn't on the peaceful morning. She could only hope she'd hidden her conflicted emotions from the little girl. Behind her, the back door opened. Just as Malory craned her head to see their guest, Katy shoved a tuna-salad finger sandwich toward her, planting the sticky mass onto her cheek. Malory laughed and turned back to Katy.

"You missed my mouth." She chuckled, reaching for a napkin.

"Missed your mouth." Katy giggled, grabbing another sandwich. "Again!"

"No, no, no." Malory managed to avoid another face full of tuna and took a bite of sandwich instead. "Yum. Look, Uncle Mike needs us."

Mike's broad frame filled up the doorway. He waved, then stepped outside and strolled across the lawn toward them.

"Ready for us?" Malory asked. She attempted to get up, but her white cotton dress caught under her sandal. Mike held out a hand. She hesitated for a moment, then slipped her fingers into his strong grip, tugging her dress free and rising to her feet.

"Having fun out here?" he asked, his expression tender.

She nodded. "Katy sure is enjoying herself. Hungry?"

On cue, Katy held up a sandwich toward Mike, compacted and flattened between her eager fingers.

"Uh—" Mike regarded the unappetizing little mass of tuna and bread. "I'm okay, thanks."

"Eat it," Katy urged. "It's for you. Eat it!"

"Hmm." Mike took the sandwich. "How about I have it later?"

"No, now."

He cast a helpless look toward Malory, who laughed, wiping her cheek once more with the napkin. "Just try and get out of that one."

Mike hesitated, then popped the mangled sandwich into his mouth, making a grimace as it went in. He chewed thoughtfully. "Not bad."

"Another one!" Katy squealed, diving for the last finger sandwich on the plate, and Malory caught her before she reached her goal.

"That's enough, sweetie." She laughed. "It's time to go say hello to someone."

"Who?" Katy asked, looking up, suddenly suspicious.

"A lady," Mike said. "She just wants to say hi. Can you say hi to a lady?"

Malory had never met a child so wise to grown-up ploys, but this child had seen a lot in her young years and seemed to sense incoming instability in her world. She clutched Malory's hand a little more tightly, her rosebud lips pressing down into a thin line.

Mike's smile didn't reach his eyes as he walked

back toward the house. She followed, her little charge in tow.

When they entered the living room, their guest stood. She smiled as she saw Katy.

"You must be Katy," she said.

Katy didn't answer.

"I've heard lots of good things about you," the woman went on. "I just wanted to meet you for myself. How old are you?"

Katy held up three fingers.

"Oh, my. That's very old." She nodded solemnly. "When is her birthday?" She looked up at Mike inquiringly.

"February 12," he said.

"She looks like a healthy child," the woman said with a smile toward Malory. "And well cared for."

"Thank you." Malory knew the compliment was meant for her as the nanny. "She's a wonderful little girl."

"Well…" The woman pulled a small digital camera out of her pocket. "Maybe I could take a picture of you, Katy?"

Katy looked at the camera dubiously and took a step back.

"After she takes the picture of you in your pretty dress, you can look at it, too," Malory said quietly. "Does that sound nice?"

Katy stared up at the camera, eyes wide and expression solemn. The woman snapped a photo, then studied its preview.

"Can we try a smile?" she asked.

Katy shook her head, but she did lean forward to look at the picture when the woman held it out for her to see.

"I think that's the best you're going to get under the circumstances," Malory said. "If you need a photo, maybe we can try to get one and email it to you later on."

"Sure, that would be fine," the woman replied. "It was very nice to meet all of you, and, Mr. Cruise, I'll be in touch."

Mike walked her to the door, and Malory stifled a sigh. It was all so matter-of-fact, this finding a home for a little girl. What would the potential families think of that solemn picture? Would they be able to see her spunk and intelligence? Would they see her sweetness? It wasn't fair that this child would be judged so quickly and likely passed over multiple times because she was past a certain age.

"Nanny Mal?" Katy whispered.

"Yes, sweetie?"

"I don't like her."

Malory sank down into a kitchen chair and pulled the little girl up onto her knees.

"You don't need to worry. Everything is fine, sweetie."

Katy laid her flaxen head against Malory's chest, and she whispered, "I'll be good. Promise."

Tears misted Malory's eyes, and she rested her cheek against Katy's silky hair. How much did this child understand?

"You are a very good girl," she reassured her. "A very, very good girl."

Mike came back into the kitchen, and when he saw them, he stopped short. "Is everything okay?" he asked.

"I don't like the lady," Katy repeated.

"No?" Mike grinned mischievously. "Well, she's gone now, so you don't have to worry. Do you like cookies?"

"Yes!" Katy sat upright and squirmed down from Malory's lap. "I like cookies. I do. I like them."

Mike chuckled and turned toward the kitchen cupboards. She watched him, the way his muscles flexed as he reached into a top cupboard, the warm glint in his eye as he shook the box of chocolate-chip cookies for Katy to see. He glanced back at Malory.

"What about you, Nanny Mal?" he asked. "Can I interest you in some cookies, too?"

"Oh, absolutely."

Whether he saw it or not, he was good with kids. More specifically, he was good with Katy, and that was what mattered most. He pulled out a plate and dropped two cookies onto it, then offered it to Katy. Katy grabbed the cookies, leaving the plate in Mike's hand.

"Mike," Malory said as Mike put a few more cookies onto the plate. "Are you sure about this?"

He glanced back and shrugged. "I'm supposed to be."

He didn't say anything else but put the plate down

on the counter between them, and they both took a cookie. Sometimes the most certainty a person could have was a chocolate-chip cookie.

Chapter Seven

That evening, Mike stood at the back door, leaning against the door frame as he watched the lengthening shadows in the backyard. The sun was low, the last of its rays no longer reaching the ground. Pink and red tinged the sky, and the birds twittered their last calls.

It had been a tiring day. After the adoption agent left, he had gone to work for an extra shift to fill in for an officer who was recovering after getting his tonsils out. Now he was back again, his uniform rumpled from a shift on patrol in the cruiser, his collar open. The house was silent—the kind of silence he was used to from before Katy's arrival. Except now it felt strange, somehow.

He glanced at his watch. It was past nine o'clock, so Katy would already be asleep. At first he'd assumed that Malory had gone to bed, too, but now as he stood in the doorway, the evening air cooling his skin, he saw her.

Malory sat with her back to the house, her legs stretched in front of her on the grass, leaning back on her arms. Her hair fell back, away from her face and down her spine. Her face was tipped upward, and she was oblivious to his presence.

I should go in and give her some time to herself, he thought, but something held him back. Maybe it was the way the breeze shifted her hair or the way she moved one foot over the top of the other. She was beautiful—not that she seemed to recognize her own allure. She looked as though her thoughts were miles away, and he wondered what was running through her mind.

That's enough, he told himself more firmly, and as he went to go in, a floorboard creaked and Malory turned, sitting up straighter, her posture more guarded.

"Hi," she said. "I didn't see you there."

Mike paused and rubbed a hand over his short hair. "Sorry. I didn't mean to intrude."

"It's no intrusion." She smiled. "I've got the baby monitor so I can listen for Katy, but other than that, I'm just enjoying the evening. Long day?"

Mike came across the grass toward her, then sank down onto his haunches. "Glad to be home. I can say that much."

She patted the lawn next to her. "Have a seat. I won't bite."

He took her up on it. The soft swell of her belly pressed against her white cotton blouse, and she idly rubbed one hand over it. A week before, he hadn't been able to even recognize that she was pregnant, but now he felt as if it was all he could see.

So much for giving her space.

"What do you think about when you watch sunsets?" Malory asked.

"I don't know." Mike shrugged. "It makes me feel small, I guess. Especially here in Montana, where the sky is so big."

"Hmm." She nodded, and the sound she made was soft and low.

"What about you?" he asked.

"I'm hoping that I'm having a girl," she said, then laughed self-consciously.

"Why's that?" he asked. "Are they easier?"

"Probably not," she admitted. "But I was the only child of a single mom, and I have a feeling I'd do better with a girl. I'd understand her better. The thought of having a boy is scary."

"Hmm." He wasn't sure what she wanted to hear, exactly. "You're really good with Katy. You'll be a good mom."

"Thanks."

"So…" He wasn't sure if he was overstepping here, but he was curious. "How will you do this?"

Malory didn't look offended. "I've given it some thought. If I could find a position where the parent didn't mind me caring for my baby at the same time as caring for the other child, it would be a good solution. It could even be beneficial for an only child having a baby around for socializing and learning to share."

"That sounds…perfect." For a moment he'd had an image in his mind of Malory staying and her tiny baby joining the household.

"Do you think so?" she asked uncertainly. "Well, hopefully I can find someone else who does, too."

"What if you stayed here?" he asked.

"But Katy isn't staying," she said softly.

"There is always the possibility that they won't find a home for her right away," he said. "I'll need help until then."

"And I'll stay until she goes."

He was relieved to hear her say that, and he liked the thought of keeping things just like this for a while. If Malory had her baby, he could find a substitute nanny for a few weeks until Malory was ready to come back to work—

His mind was already working through the logistics. If they couldn't find a better family, would it be so terrible to keep things just like this?

Malory was quiet for a moment. Then she whispered, "I'm afraid of getting attached, you know."

So was he, but he wasn't thinking too far into the future. He just didn't want to let this end just yet. A wisp of her hair fluttered free and fell in front of her eyes. He moved it back, the silky strands falling over his finger. Yeah, he was getting attached.

"Oh!" She looked down at her stomach, and the moment disappeared. "I think I felt a kick."

"Really?"

"Do you want to feel?"

He paused for a moment, uncertain what to say. She was his employee, after all, but some lines were blurring. Before he could stop her, Malory took his hand and placed it lightly on her belly. He felt nothing but her gentle warmth under his palm and her smooth, cool fingers on top of his. Her face was close to his, her long lashes nearly brushing her cheeks as she looked down at his broad tanned hand on her soft white shirt. She smelled of floral shampoo, mingling with the lilac bushes, making him wish he could move in closer and inhale the scent of her.

"Oh, that was a big one. Did you feel it?" she asked with a low laugh, seemingly unaware of just how close he was to her.

"No." He cleared his throat, and while he knew he should pull back, he couldn't quite bring himself to do it.

She looked up at him then, and he slid his hand off her belly, away from her slender, cool fingers, but his eyes stayed fixed to her creamy complexion in the moonlight.

"It might be too early to feel it on the outside," she said apologetically.

They fell into silence. If he were honest with himself, he'd known the minute he saw her that it would be complicated.

"I was hoping for an older nanny, you know," he admitted.

"Older?" she asked. "Do you think I'm not experienced enough?"

"Not that, but I wouldn't be sitting out here with a sixty-year-old knitter, would I?"

She laughed. "You never know."

"Oh, I do." He wasn't sitting out here for the company. He was well used to spending his evenings alone, even enjoyed it. A Vin Diesel movie or a trip to the gym could hurry an evening right along. Instead, he was sitting out here on the lush green grass, his arm brushing the arm of a beautiful woman who made him think about everything but knitting.

Stars twinkled through the darkness, and Malory shivered. He knew what he wanted to do. He wanted to put an arm around those slender shoulders and pull her against him. He wanted to slide his hand onto her belly again and feel the movement inside her, and he wanted to dip his head down and catch her lips with his—

But he knew better.

"It's getting chilly," he said instead, and he pushed himself to his feet and held out a hand to her. "Ready to head in?"

"I think so," she agreed, accepting his help. He pulled her to her feet, but once she was up, she twisted her hand from his grip, and the few inches between them suddenly felt like too much.

They crossed the lawn, her sandals, held by the straps, swinging at her side. They walked up the few steps to the back door, and she hesitated. He stopped, his hand on the knob.

"Mike?" she asked, and they paused there in the cool evening.

"Hmm?" He looked down into her eyes, the golden light from the window reflected in them. His gaze moved to her pink lips, parted ever so slightly, then back to those deep brown eyes...

"Are you hungry, too?" she asked. "Because I'm famished, and I'm not sure if it's just me."

Mike burst out laughing and shook his head. He reached out and opened the door, the warmth from inside flooding out to meet them.

"No," he admitted. "Not really. But I make a great sandwich. Come on. Let's feed you."

He was more attracted to her than he'd cared to admit before, and now that he knew it, he'd have to be a whole lot more careful. She was not only his employee, but she was also pregnant and vulnerable. There was no way he was going to be the guy who took advantage of her when she needed support the most.

As THEY CAME inside the kitchen, Malory let out a little sigh. Had she wanted him to kiss her? She wasn't even sure right now. Of course, wanting him to kiss her and being willing to be kissed—by anyone—were two different things, and she was trying very hard to keep her life together and uncomplicated. A baby was complication enough.

"What kind of sandwich do you want?" Mike asked, opening the fridge. "We've got ham, roast beef or salami. Or if you're really patient, I can boil a couple of eggs and make egg salad—"

"Oh, I can make it myself," she said.

"Didn't say you couldn't," he replied. "But it's my kitchen, so I've decided to get all territorial."

Malory laughed. "Well, if you insist on using that card, then I suppose I'll have ham and cheese."

"Good choice." Mike set to work.

"About that older nanny—" Malory began.

"I was just joking around." He grabbed a loaf of

bread from the counter. "You're every bit a professional."

"But would it be more comfortable living with an older woman in the house?" she asked.

Mike paused, then let his gaze meet hers. "Well, I'll put it this way—she wouldn't remind me of what I was missing quite so much."

Malory felt a blush rise in her cheeks. "Not so happy with the single life?"

"I wouldn't say that, exactly." He turned back to the sandwich making, and Malory mentally kicked herself for the personal question. Frankly, it didn't matter if he enjoyed his single status or not—she wasn't about to help him change it.

"I told you about my mother," Malory said. "She was always searching for her Mr. Right."

"Did she ever find him?" Mike asked.

"Not yet," Malory said. "You never know what the future holds, though. She's been dating a nice guy for a while."

"You really resent all those boyfriends coming and going, don't you?" he asked, bringing the sandwich to her.

"I did for a long time." She accepted the plate with a smile. "My mom was afraid to be alone. She thought that being single meant that she wasn't worth anything—no one wanted her."

"That's sad."

"Really sad," Malory agreed. "I just don't see it that way. I'd rather be a good mother than in a relationship."

Her mother had done her best, and Malory was her

mother's biggest champion. But it seemed that all too often, her mother's boyfriends had sidled their way into being the highest priority, their whims and demands trumping Malory's needs. She was sure that her mother had never intended for that to happen, but it had.

"I really respect that." He picked up the bread and clipped the bag shut again. "My parents wouldn't have won any awards, so when someone puts their child ahead of their own desires—" He cleared his throat. "I guess I'm trying to say that I think you'll make a good mom."

"Thanks." They were silent for a moment. Then Malory picked up her sandwich—ham and cheese on fluffy white bread. His gaze lingered on her while she took a big bite. The tang of mayonnaise and pickles mingled with salty ham, and she sighed happily.

"But what if you didn't have to choose between being a good mom and having some romance?" Mike broke the quiet. "What would you want then?"

"I don't know," she replied, dabbing her lips with a napkin. "I can really only look at what I need right now."

"Which is?"

"A job. Health insurance. A stable home for my baby once she's born." She took another bite and, after she swallowed, added, "And this sandwich—how do you make it so good?"

Mike grinned. "What can I say? It's a gift."

"I think sometimes we get afraid of repeating our parents' mistakes. I know I do," she said and licked a daub of mayo off her fingertip.

"You don't seem like the type to look to a man to complete you," he said. "I wouldn't worry too much."

Her mother had higher ideals, too, right after every breakup. She'd swear off men indefinitely and then meet another one. She'd judged her mother rather harshly when she was younger, but she had more sympathy now.

"It doesn't take away that tiny nagging worry that I'll somehow slip down the slope, you know?"

"Yeah, I know." He nodded, his dark gaze turning inward for a moment.

She had a feeling he was thinking of his own family's slippery slopes. "For the record, you aren't like your dad, either."

"I'm not an addict. That's one point in my favor," he said bitterly.

"No, but more than that. You were pretty much neglected as a child, but you're not that kind of guy. With a surprise child in your home, you've stepped up. That really says a lot about who you are."

He met her gaze for a moment, then said, "One day maybe I'll be able to give it a whirl—being a dad, that is."

Malory could easily imagine Mike as a father with his gentle strength and infectious grin. The woman who ended up with him would be lucky. She'd have the life that most women only dreamed of—a strong, sexy husband devoted to her and their children. Who didn't want the white picket fence in a little town called Hope?

"It makes me wonder what my own child will see

as my shortcomings," she said at last. "I'm sure I'll have a few."

"Don't we all." Mike leaned against the counter and crossed his muscular arms over his chest.

Sitting here in this beautiful kitchen close to a sheriff with a heart of gold, she could understand her mother's desire for love, at least.

Her mother had wanted that happy home, loving husband and safe place to raise her children, and she'd looked in the only place she'd known to look—with a man. Somehow, in this house that would never be hers, looking into the open face of a man who would also never be hers, she understood that desire to grab what she could.

Except Malory was different from her mother— not better, just different. She understood her mother's dreams more now that she was about to become a single mother herself, but she also knew what it was like to be the child in that situation. She hadn't needed a father figure in her life as much as she'd needed her mother's stability and strength.

Watching her mother struggle with her own self-worth, looking for her answers in a relationship, Malory had learned her most important lesson between the lines: if she was to be the mother she needed to be, she needed to be her own answer.

Malory finished the sandwich and smiled at Mike. "Thank you," she said. "This was delicious."

"Anytime."

She brought the plate to the sink and looked up at

her boss. "Mike, I think we might count as friends at this point."

"I think we might." He tilted his head. "Are you okay with that?"

"Definitely." She stifled a yawn. "But I'm really tired and I'm fading fast."

"You should get some rest," he said. "I'll clean up down here."

"Thanks." She felt another surge of that longing, but she cleared her throat and dropped her gaze. "Good night."

"Good night, Nanny Mal."

She made her way up to her bedroom. Fairy tales had princesses and knights, castles and true love. Real life had jobs, insurance, surprise babies and some hard-won wisdom in the mix. While she sometimes wished for a castle to protect her and a knight to defend her, real life didn't rely on potions and fairy godmothers. Real life was about the simple things—hard work, dependability and putting one foot in front of the other.

If there was one thing she knew how to do, it was put one foot in front of the other.

Chapter Eight

A few days later, Malory sat in her bedroom, bathed in the soft glow of her bedside lamp. It had been a busy day with Katy. They'd done some shopping for new clothes and bought a little pink comb that Katy had chosen herself. No more brushes for her. They'd stopped by the park to play and then come home to make supper and have a bath. Malory had shown Katy how to comb her own hair, and before she knew it, the day was gone, and Malory sat alone upstairs, listening to the wind whispering through the leaves of the trees. She lay propped up on her bed, pillows behind her.

Mike was working a night shift again, and while she was partly relieved not to be left alone with the handsome cop, the house did feel cavernous without him.

"I don't know what to tell you, Mom," she said into her cell phone. "He's a good boss, but I certainly don't want to complicate things."

"What's life without a little complication?" her mother replied with a laugh. "I always dated."

"I know." Malory attempted to keep her tone neutral. "Regardless, it's a good thing that he's gone tonight. The other night was just a little bit too tempting."

"And how is the baby?" her mother asked, a smile in her voice.

"She's kicking right now." Malory put her hand on her expanding waistline. It seemed almost unreal most days, and when she looked at herself in the mirror, she stared at her new shape, mesmerized.

"Oh...I remember that feeling. Remember it, Mal. You'll think back on all of this for years."

Malory rubbed her belly. "I have an ultrasound booked to find out the gender this week. I'm so nervous about it. I don't even know why. I'm lucky I got an appointment so quickly—they had a cancellation and managed to squeeze me in."

"Oh, don't be nervous. It'll be exciting to find out if this is a boy or a girl," her mother said. "You have to tell me right away so I know what color of sleepers to start buying." There was a pause. "Can I convince you to come home a little early?"

"I've promised Mike that I'll stay here as long as he needs me," she replied. "But when this job is done, I'll be on the next plane."

"Do you have any idea when that will be?"

Malory sighed. "He's looking for a new family for her. It might be a few weeks. I might be a few months. Maybe more."

"I hope it isn't selfish, but I'm crossing my fingers for sooner."

"I've missed you, too, Mom."

"Actually, it won't just be you and me... I have some news."

"Oh? What's going on?"

"Ted asked me to marry him."

"What?" Malory clamped a hand over her mouth and lowered her voice. "Are you serious? When did this happen?"

"Last night." Her mother let out a happy sigh. "He took me out to our favorite restaurant—you know the fish place, right?"

"Yes, of course. How did he ask?" Outside, something thumped, and Malory stood up, shading her eyes and peering down into the backyard. Everything seemed silent and still.

"Down on one knee!" her mother gushed. "He had one of his friends come and play a violin for us—not very well, since the guy is just starting lessons. I think it was 'Three Blind Mice.' But it was still really sweet, and then he got down on his knee—which was no easy feat with his bad leg—and he said, 'Shelly,' he said, 'you know what I'm asking. So what do you say?'"

Malory laughed and shook her head. "Straight to the point."

"Isn't he always? So I said yes," her mother went on. "And I think I cried a bit. My mascara was a mess when I got home. He hasn't gotten me a ring yet. It was either get a diamond now and put off the wedding or get married right away. So we're getting married just as soon as you're back."

"Mom, that's amazing news." Malory couldn't help the smile on her face. "You deserve this."

"Thanks, sweetie. Ted really is worth the wait. He's one of the good ones."

"And he's moving in now?" she asked.

"Of course! But he's perfectly thrilled that you're coming back, too. He says he always wanted kids, so a grandbaby will just warm him right through."

Misgivings welled up inside her. The thought of raising this baby with her mother at her side was a relief—but with Ted, too? Somehow, the homey feel was evaporating in her imagination, replaced with irritation and foreboding. Another thump and a scrape drew her attention out the window once more, and she squinted, looking for the source of the noise.

"But, Mom, do you think this is going to work? I mean, babies cry. A lot. And your place is small."

"What would you suggest?" her mother asked.

"That I get a different place on my own. I'll have to eventually, and I'll only have the six weeks off before I go back to work—"

"You couldn't afford anything decent, and I won't have you in some dive somewhere. Think about the baby."

"I suppose there is time to talk about it, and don't let me ruin the moment. Look, Mom, I'm really happy for you."

A smash and the tinkle of broken glass froze Malory's blood. She held her breath, listening. The back door opened, and footfalls tapped against the tiled floor.

"Mom," she whispered hoarsely. "I think someone's breaking in!"

"What?" her mother shrieked. "Call the police! What are you waiting for?"

Malory hung up the call and crept out of the bedroom and into the shadowy hallway. Downstairs, boots crunched over glass shards, but no lights went on. Everything was inky darkness. She tiptoed to Katy's door and eased it open with a creak. She winced, listened. Silence now, except for the hammering of her heart. Someone was definitely inside the house, and she was willing to bet that the intruder was listening just as carefully as she was.

She could feel tears of fear welling up. But she didn't dare let them fall. Malory sneaked into Katy's bedroom, her breath coming in shaky gasps. Katy slept on peacefully, and Malory dialed her cell phone with a trembling hand.

"911. What is the nature of your emergency?"

"I'm at 2032 Boundary Road," she whispered into the phone. "There is an intruder in the house."

"Are you alone, miss?"

"Yes, me and a little girl." She put a hand on Katy, who squirmed, blinking her eyes open tiredly. "Someone broke a window, and now they're inside—"

"Stay quiet and calm. Are you somewhere safe?"

"I'm in the upstairs bedroom," she hissed. "I'm Mike Cruise's nanny. He's a sheriff here in Hope."

"Yes, ma'am. I've already signaled the police and they're already on their way. Are you with the child now?"

"Yes, we're together."

"Then stay on the line. Help is on the way."

Stay on the line. A phone somehow didn't feel very protective right now.

"Nanny Mal?" Katy asked, her voice quavering.

Malory suppressed the urge to cover Katy's mouth. It would only make the child panic. Instead, she whispered,

"Shh... Let's play a game. We're going to be very, very quiet, okay?"

Katy stared at Malory, eyes wide with fear. She wasn't fooled. She looked as if she was about to cry. Malory pulled the girl onto her lap and smoothed her hair down.

"It's okay. I'm here with you," she whispered. "You don't need to worry. And there is a lady on the phone who is getting the police..."

Malory strained to listen. As long as the burglar stayed downstairs until the police arrived, that was all that Malory cared about. She looked around the room. They couldn't just stay out in the open here, waiting for the intruder to find them.

"We're going to the closet, okay? We're going to hide."

Katy clung to her as Malory crept toward the closet. A floorboard creaked and she froze, listening. The footsteps downstairs stopped, then changed directions. Shoes clomped as they hit the stairs.

"He's coming upstairs," Malory gasped into the phone. "He's coming up!"

The closet door was already open, and Malory pushed Katy inside first, then slipped into the darkness, tugging the door shut behind her. It wouldn't close all the way, and Malory pushed farther back into the piles of old clothes, a cardboard box digging into her side. She put one arm around Katy. Pulling the phone back up to her ear, she listened to the soft voice on the other end.

"The police have arrived. Stay quiet. They're already on the scene."

Malory nearly melted with relief, and warm tears spilled silently down her cheeks. She couldn't hear the cops—she heard only those ominous footsteps moving down the hallway, doors opening and the footsteps coming ever closer.

"Nanny Mal…" Katy whimpered, and Malory pulled her face into her side.

"Shh," she whispered, Katy's tears wetting her shirt. She pulled Katy closer, holding her breath as she listened.

The door to the bedroom opened.

MIKE TOOK A LONG step to the side, avoiding the shards of glass that would give away his presence.

Unbuckling the safety strap on his gun harness, he slid the Glock 9 millimeter from the holster, the weight of the sidearm familiar in his palm. He knew this gun inside and out, and on the practice range he shot with precision.

Tuck slipped into the house behind him, and Mike glanced back, gesturing him forward into the living room while Mike slipped into the downstairs hallway. The only damage seemed to be to the door so far, and he couldn't see signs that the intruder had rifled through his belongings.

But it wasn't his belongings he cared about—he was thinking of the girls. The 911 operator had said that a woman and child were on premises, and he was going to get to them before this creep did.

Moving silently forward, he came to the staircase, and a floorboard creaked under his weight. He halted. Tuck whipped around, pistol pointed at Mike before he heaved a silent sigh and eased his finger off the trigger. Mike took the stairs two at a time, his firearm aimed in front of him, his palm under the butt of the gun as he stole swiftly up the stairs and into the dim hallway.

The light in Malory's room was on, and he glanced inside to find it empty. Katy's room next door stood open, and he stopped at the doorway. The perp was in his sights, but so far, he couldn't see Malory or Katy.

The man wore black, a knit cap on his head, a gun hanging in his hand. He stood in the center of the room, slowly turning.

Looking for them, he realized with a chill in his blood.

"Good evening," Mike said, his tone casual and light—a distinct contrast to the gun he had pointed at the perp's chest.

The man spun around, and Mike almost laughed when he recognized who it was standing in his house, armed. His father—thin and wiry, face lined with the deep furrows of a hard life.

"I haven't taken anything," his father said. "I'm putting the gun down—"

"That's probably wise," he replied. "Kick it this way."

His father bent and put the gun on the floor.

"Slowly, now," Mike crooned.

He kicked it in Mike's direction, then put his hands on his head. "It's me, Mikey. It's Dad."

"Yeah, I know," Mike replied. He pulled out a set of cuffs from his back pocket, strode forward and secured his father before patting him down. He found one more gun and a knife sheathed along his calf. "But you seem to have a lot of weapons for a little family visit, wouldn't you say?"

Mike scanned the room, and his gaze stopped at the closet. Were they in there? Were they okay? Malory's ashen face appeared beside the closet door.

"Hey." He heard his tone soften as he grinned at the nanny. "You girls okay?"

"We're fine…" But the tears on her face told him otherwise. She was terrified.

Tuck's footsteps thundered up the stairs. Then he came into the room behind them. "The house is secure. Everything under control here?"

"Yeah, get the light."

Light flooded the room when Tuck flipped the wall switch, and Mike nudged his father toward Tuck. "Book him, would you?"

"You bet." Tuck put a hand under his father's arm and led him to the door. "You have the right to remain silent. By the way, it's nice to see you, Nate. You have the right to an attorney…"

Only when his father was in Tuck's capable hands did Mike let down his guard and holster his gun.

"Your father?" Malory gasped, crawling slowly from the closet. Mike bent down and put his hands under her arms, lifting her to her feet. She bent over slightly, her arm protectively over her belly.

"You okay?" he asked.

"Just some cramping." She grimaced. "The stress, I think."

"Here, sit on Katy's bed." He helped her over to the bed, then held out his hand for Katy, who crawled out of the closet and immediately attached herself to his leg. They both looked pale and drawn, and anger simmered inside him when he thought of how frightened they must have been.

"That's your father?" Malory repeated, and she held out her arms to Katy, who released Mike and clambered up onto her lap.

"Yeah." He scanned the room again, his mind on the task at hand. He was looking for clues—some indication of what his father had been after. When his gaze came back around to Malory, she was wiping fresh tears from her cheeks.

"Sorry." He sank onto the bed next to her and put an arm around her tense shoulders. "I have no idea what he was doing breaking into my house, but yes, that's my father. You don't need to worry, though. I'll get to the bottom of this."

"I thought we'd be killed—" Her voice broke off into a rough sob, and Mike pulled her against his shoulder, her tears leaving a warm wet spot on his uniform.

"Not on my watch, babe," he murmured, then stopped when he realized the endearment that had slipped from his lips.

Malory seemed to put some effort into reining in her tears, and she gave Katy a shaky smile, wiping the child's hair away from her face. Mike cleared his throat, then stood up, glancing out the window where cops were set up, measuring and taking pictures for the inevitable trial.

"In fact, I'm going to go interrogate him now. The house is safe."

"Yes, of course." Malory sucked in a ragged breath. "Go do your job."

"Are you going to be okay?" he asked, looking back at her. He hated to leave them like this, terrified and tear streaked, but he couldn't just sit still, either, while there were answers to demand downstairs.

"I'll be fine."

He didn't entirely believe her, and he was more than aware that all of this had been caused by his own father. The Cruises at their finest.

A female officer came into the room, and Mike smiled gratefully. "Sheila, good timing. Would you stay with Malory for a bit while I go do a little personal interrogating?"

"You bet," Sheila replied, coming into the room and standing with her legs akimbo. Sheila was probably tougher than most guys on the force. In fact, she could outbox Tuck—a little detail Mike never could let Tuck live down.

"You're in good hands, Malory," he said, catching her eye.

He wished he could stay, but he felt responsible for this. His father was back in town for a reason, and he should have gotten to the bottom of it before…this. It wasn't right that Malory and Katy should be terrified in his home. They should be safe here, of all places… but wasn't this what he'd been afraid of all along? Katy wouldn't be free so long as anyone knew where she was. Right now Mike had one thing on his mind, and he trotted down the stairs to where his father sat, cuffed and sullen, in the middle of the living room floor.

"Thought you might want to question him before we brought him back to the station," Tuck said.

"Thanks." Mike glanced around at the other officers, and they moved back, giving him some space. He sat on the edge of the couch, facing the older man. "So."

"Mike, it isn't what it looks like," his father sputtered. "I swear."

"Yeah? Well, it looks like you broke into my house and scared Malory and Katy out of their minds. That's not what happened here?" His voice dripped with sarcasm.

"I wasn't going to hurt them." He shifted his position. Those cuffs were tight—Mike had made sure of that. "I'm in a bit of a situation."

"So you didn't just call to say hi after all," Mike retorted.

"Look, after talking to you, I knew you'd never give me any money. And I needed it. Bad."

"Bad enough to break into my house?" Mike snapped.

"I knew you were working. I called the station just to be sure. It was better than someone else's house."

"Counting on my forgiving nature?" Mike snapped.

"Sort of, yeah," his father replied. "Look, I owe some money, and the guy I owe it to will kill me if I don't pay up."

"How much are we talking?" Mike asked.

"Ten grand."

"That's more than you could steal in my house," Mike said. "And what about these?" He lifted the guns and knife to eye level.

"Just a little protection."

"So you break into my house armed to the teeth, and I'm supposed to believe you weren't going to use them?" Mike demanded.

"No. Not like that. These guys who are after me are dangerous. It's self-defense, I swear."

"And what exactly did you hope to take from my place that would be worth ten grand on the black market?"

"I've got some of the money," his father replied, shifting again uncomfortably. "Just not all. I'm desperate here."

"So just out of wild curiosity," Mike said, his tone flat, "what kind of debt is this? Gambling? Drugs?"

"Gambling."

"Ah." Mike sighed and ran a hand through his hair. "Well, you were right the first time. I'm not giving you a cent, but I'm also not setting you loose."

"What are you gonna do with me?" his father asked warily.

"You've already been arrested, Dad. I'm putting you in lockup. You're facing trial. I can't get you out of this one."

"Trial?" His father gasped. "With my record, they'll put me away for twenty years!"

"Probably." Mike shrugged. "But I'm pretty ticked off right now, and I'm not bubbling over with sympathy." In fact, he was barely containing his rage, and he wanted to make his father pay for every single tear that Malory and Katy had shed up there while they'd hunched in terror in a closet.

He rose to his feet and beckoned to his partner, who stood across the room, pretending not to listen. "Tuck, you can take him back to the station."

Tuck nodded. "Sure thing, Mike. Ready to go, Nate?"

"I get the feeling you're enjoying this," Nate grumbled, and Tuck shrugged.

"A bit." He chuckled. "Hey, we all know you, Nate. It's a bit of a reunion, wouldn't you say?"

"Wait—" Nate turned back and stumbled a step when Tuck kept moving. "Wait."

"What?" Mike demanded, his tone like gravel.

"I've got a woman in my life—Gina. She'll worry. I told her I was visiting family."

"And she believed you?" Mike said, then sighed. "I'll let you have two calls—Gina and your attorney."

"Thanks, kid." Nate nodded and allowed himself to be led out the door.

Mike crossed his arms over his chest. He wasn't going to stop until he got to the bottom of whatever was going on here. He knew for a fact that his father wasn't telling everything—Cruises never told everything.

He also knew that Malory and Katy were no longer safe. This was more than a break-in—this had just turned personal.

Chapter Nine

That night, the only one who could get to sleep was Katy, but that was because she was snuggled up in Malory's arms. Malory got up to investigate every sound, and each time, she found Mike up, talking on his radio to the cops patrolling, or looking out a window into the darkness.

By morning, Malory was pretty sure she wasn't looking her best, but her back was sore from sleeping scrunched in Katy's bed. So she carefully slid her arm out from underneath the sleeping girl and yawned.

Morning sunlight streamed into the room from the crack in the curtains, and as Malory scooted off the bed, Katy sighed in her sleep and rolled over onto her back, damp curls sticking to her forehead. In the morning light, everything was normal again. The drama of the night before seemed more like a dream.

She moved a curl off Katy's forehead. Life had been hard enough on this little girl, but she understood now why Mike was so insistent that Katy go to another family. He knew best.

Downstairs, she could make out the pop and sizzle

of bacon frying, and her stomach rumbled. The house was quiet, and she shook her head. What was it about Hope, Montana, that absorbed the chaos and left everything feeling as pure and sweet as ever?

"Morning," she said as she shuffled into the kitchen, and Mike looked over his shoulder, a forkful of bacon dripping fat back into the pan.

"How'd you sleep?" he asked.

"Horribly, but not as badly as you. I don't think you slept at all."

"I catnapped. It was enough."

Malory gave him a sympathetic smile. "Are you off to work?"

"That's not exactly how this works," he replied, half smiling in return. "I'm assigned to you."

"To me?"

"Well, to both you and Katy. I'm your escort until we figure out what's going on here."

"Escort?" Malory frowned. "Is it as serious as all that?"

"Don't know." He slid the plate of bacon across the counter toward her. "But I'm not about to take any chances."

"I know what you mean now about your father." An image had been tattooed on her brain of the man standing in the middle of Katy's darkened bedroom, a gun held casually in one hand. She shivered.

Mike grimaced. "Desperate people do desperate things. They don't have to be evil to the core to be dangerous, just backed into a corner."

Dangerous was exactly how she'd describe Nate Cruise—very dangerous.

"And you think your father is backed into a corner?"

"Without a doubt."

"Are we safe now?" she asked, looking nervously toward the door, its broken window taped over with cardboard.

"There are some cruisers patrolling, my dad is in lockup and I'm here with you two. I think you can relax."

Malory took a crisp strip of bacon and munched for a moment, savoring the salty perfection. Mike turned back to the pan and cracked in a couple of eggs.

"So what did your dad say?" she asked.

"That he owes a rather bad man some money." Mike's tone didn't change. He might as well have been announcing that it was going to rain that day.

"So why was he here?"

"He claimed he was going to rob me."

"And you don't believe him?"

"Even if he sold every piece of furniture I own, he couldn't have come up with that kind of cash, so I don't exactly trust his story right now."

Malory nodded slowly. "Do you think this is about Katy somehow?"

"I don't know what to think. I should probably go have a chat with my cousin Crystal, though, one of these days soon. She might know something."

He sounded as if he were simply making morning conversation, but underneath it all, she sensed the tension. These people were his family—his blood relatives—and he couldn't trust a word that came from their lips. He seemed so different from that world, so honorable and kind, yet she could tell that his link to them chafed him.

Mike busied himself with the eggs. "Don't worry about it," he said.

"Easier said than done," she retorted. "Last night I was crouching in a closet, calling 911."

"I know." He winced. "And I can't begin to tell you how sorry I am for that." His expression grew grim. "I know you like to take care of yourself. I get that. I even respect it. But right now keeping you safe is my job."

"Good!"

He closed the space between them, reaching up to push a strand of hair away from her eyes. The gentle gesture stood in stark contrast with the grate in his voice. "I want you to do exactly as I tell you when I tell you to do it. If I say to drop to the ground, you take Katy and you flatten yourselves against that floor. If I say run, you run. If I say come, you come. Got it?"

She eyed him cautiously.

"As soon as this is cleared up, I'll back right off, I swear," he said, his steely eyes locked on hers. "But right now your life might depend on it."

"Okay," she whispered.

"Good." He relaxed but only slightly. "Because if something happened to you, I'd turn into one of those damaged, angry cops who drinks too much."

"Damaged?"

He put a finger under her chin, tilting her face upward, his dark eyes smoldering down into hers. "It wouldn't be pretty. So just cooperate, okay?"

She felt a little weak-kneed looking up into those eyes. He leaned closer, so close that she could feel the warmth of his breath against her face. He ran a finger down her cheek, then pressed his soft lips against hers in a brief kiss.

"Just be careful, okay?" He glanced back out the window. "By the way, that cooperating thing needs to start now."

Dread dropped into the center of Malory's stomach. "What's wrong?"

"Someone's out there. I want you to go upstairs with the phone and stay with Katy until I give you the all clear."

Malory's heart hammered in her throat, and she nodded quickly. "Okay."

And with that, he pulled a gun from his back holster and slipped out the back door, closing it behind him with a soft click. Malory bolted for the stairs.

MIKE EDGED AROUND the house and pulled out his radio.

"This is Sheriff Cruise requesting backup," he murmured into the radio. Then he dialed down the volume and tucked it back onto his belt, not waiting for an answer. They heard him, and they'd respond—he could count on that.

As he crept along the edge of the house, he mentally kicked himself. He was comfortable chasing down bad guys. He was built for this kind of thing. He'd always been athletic and at ease with his body, but his heart was another matter completely.

I never should have kissed her. What he'd been thinking, he had no idea. He hadn't been thinking—that was the problem. He'd wanted to kiss her a little more passionately than he had, but a kiss was a kiss. Bosses didn't kiss employees. Sheriffs didn't kiss the civilians they were charged with protecting.

A stick snapped under his shoe, and he stopped, scanning the yard in front of the house. Empty. He'd seen someone quite clearly in his backyard, and he wasn't given to imagining things. He angled his steps across the yard and surveyed the street. Nothing.

"Where are you?" he muttered under his breath, then headed around the other side of the house. Everything looked calm and peaceful.

Was he getting paranoid? The chief had seemed to think so—until he saw exactly how armed Nate had been. That had sparked his suspicions, as well. But Mike was now responsible for a little girl and her nanny. If it were just him, he might have simply waited it out to see if anyone else would make a move. But it wasn't just him anymore, and he wasn't exactly sure how to do this "family man" routine.

And I'm making myself look like an idiot.

Heading back toward the house, he saw it—a flash of red in the scraggly bushes by the kitchen window. He pulled aside the branches to reveal a faded baseball cap snagged on a branch.

"And that wasn't there last night." He knew that for

a fact. He'd checked this area himself three times, and it had been gone over by two other officers, too.

"I shouldn't be so self-congratulatory," he reminded himself. He didn't want to be proven right.

He picked up the hat and slapped it against his palm. He didn't have a detailed enough description to pass along for the cruisers, but at least he knew he wasn't getting soft.

He went back inside and headed up the stairs.

"All clear," he called.

He could hear Katy in the bedroom chattering about a tea party. Stopping at the doorway, he felt himself smile when he saw the girl pouring a pretend cup of tea for her nanny.

"Everything okay?" Malory asked. Her face was pale, and her eyes were wide with anxiety.

"Yeah, it's fine."

"Was someone out there?" she pressed.

"Not anymore." He shot her what he hoped was a reassuring smile. "Nothing to worry about."

"Ready for breakfast?" Malory asked Katy a little too brightly, and the girl bounded from the bedroom.

Mike cleared his throat as Malory rose to her feet.

"Look. About before…"

"No, it's fine," she said quickly, but she didn't meet his gaze, a blush blooming in her cheeks.

"I mean, I shouldn't have done that—kissed you, I mean. I don't know what I was thinking."

"It was just a weird situation," she said with a quick shake of her head. "It's forgotten. It never happened."

She rushed past him and out into the hallway, leav-

ing him alone in the bedroom with the lingering scent
of that floral perfume.

"Idiot," he muttered to himself. He'd made her uncomfortable. He'd crossed a line. He had to pull things
together and stop this foolishness. Obviously, he was
getting more attached than he'd realized, and it was
time to rein his feelings in. Kissing her was one mistake he wouldn't be making again.

As MALORY HEADED down the stairs, her heart felt sodden, as if she could wring it out into a puddle on the
floor. She felt filled to the brim with heavy emotion
that she didn't know what to do with.

We're fine. We're safe, she reminded herself, but she
knew it wasn't only the break-in that was nagging at
her. It was that kiss. Mike had been right—he'd overstepped.

The gesture had been sweet, but it also reminded her
a little too vividly of the boyfriend who had up and left,
breaking her heart and callously denying their child in
one fell swoop. Steve had kissed her tenderly. Steve
had cared about her comfort—until one day when he
simply hadn't anymore.

She'd been so wrapped up with her pregnancy that
she'd pushed those feelings aside, but when it came
right down to it, she didn't want to feel overly safe.
She didn't want to feel overly protected. It was better
to be rational and look out for herself. That way, she'd
stay strong and confident instead of being rocked to
the core when things didn't work out the way she ex-

pected. It was reckless to get used to something that wasn't going to last anyway.

She might not always be something special to a man, but she would always be a mother, and that was the role she was going to hold on to.

Mike came into the kitchen behind them and she turned away. The eggs were ruined, so she reached for the cereal that was irritatingly just out of reach. The entire kitchen was geared for the tall sheriff, not for his petite nanny.

"Need a hand?"

She hoped her tight smile came across as professional. "Please."

Mike moved up behind her, the warmth emanating from him as he brought the boxes of cereal down.

"Thanks." She headed back to the table.

"You mad at me?" he asked cautiously.

"Not at all." She filled a little bowl for Katy, then headed back to the fridge for the milk. He stepped back as she swept by. It was the truth—she wasn't angry, just more vulnerable than she'd thought.

"You sure about that?" There was humor in his tone, which served only to irritate her more.

"Absolutely positive," she snapped. "I think I'd know."

She didn't want to rely on Mike, or to get used to his gruff protectiveness. It felt too nice, and it wasn't a permanent arrangement. It was like giving a poor kid a night in a mansion—some things were better left alone if you were going to be happy with your life.

She poured the milk over Katy's cereal, then pushed

it gently toward the little girl. Katy sank her spoon happily into her bowl and took a big, dribbling bite.

"So..." Mike grabbed his own bowl from the cupboard and joined them. "You said you have a doctor's appointment tomorrow?"

"An ultrasound," she replied.

"Are you going to find out the sex of the baby?" he asked, eyebrows raised in interest, and she turned to meet his gaze for the first time.

"Yes," she said simply. "I'm going to see if my maternal instinct is right or not."

He wouldn't understand how deep those words ran, she knew. Being a mom was all she had left, and she could only hope that she'd be good at it. Her first personal test of motherhood was this one—her instincts about the baby inside her. The feeling that this baby was a girl had blossomed into something bigger, something more insistent...and she was terrified of being wrong.

She needed to be right about something. And that was something that she doubted Mike would be able to understand.

Chapter Ten

The next morning, Malory checked her watch for the umpteenth time since they'd started out for the medical clinic in the neighboring town. The morning had been hectic. Malory had started getting Katy ready early, but everything had gone wrong. There had been two full tantrums from Katy, a change of clothes, and then after everyone was loaded up into Mike's truck, Katy had announced that she needed to use the bathroom so Malory had dashed her back inside.

By the time they finally started driving, they were twenty minutes behind, and Malory could only pray that they'd arrive on time. Stressing out wasn't going to help the situation, and she tried to calm her already frayed nerves.

"Nanny Mal, am I coming with you?" Katy asked from the backseat.

"You'll stay with Uncle Mike," Malory said for the fourth time, glancing back at the little girl. "I just have to go for an appointment."

"But I want to go," Katy implored. "I don't wanna stay with Uncle Mike."

"Aren't you happy you get to come for the ride?" Malory asked, infusing extra cheerfulness into her tone. "Rides are fun. We can look out the window and count all the cows we can see."

"I like cows," Katy declared.

"Me, too," Malory replied. "So let's look for cows, okay?"

"So this is what it's like to get somewhere with a child, huh?" Mike asked with a chuckle.

"Afraid so," she agreed. "I really hope I don't miss my appointment. It was a miracle to get slotted in so quickly as it was."

"I could always slap a siren on the roof, if you need me to."

Malory smiled. She wasn't sure if he was joking or not, but if pressed, she might take him up on that. She glanced out the window at the looping power lines that stretched alongside the road over the flat open plains. Everything looked so small out here in Montana—tiny roads spiderwebbing across vast green stretches. Everyone drove a truck, but even the large vehicles were dwarfed by the landscape. Land rolled on as far as the eye could see, and the sky domed over it, even bigger than that endless land. Green wheat rippled across the fields, cradled by lopsided barbed-wire fences. The dark shadows of clouds moved over the fields, the great mounds of cumulous cotton sailing across the blue sky faster than seemed possible.

Katy clunked a toy against her car seat. The exit ramp brought them into the town of Rickton, and the GPS on the dash gave them polite verbal directions to-

ward the clinic. Rickton looked like any other town in
this county, just bigger. They had a few chain restaurants, a good-sized hotel and a small shopping mall.
Malory glanced at her watch and inwardly groaned.
They were already fifteen minutes late.

The clinic was located in a strip mall between a
flower shop and a used bookstore, and the parking lot
was surprisingly busy for this time of day. Rickton
seemed to be a bustling little metropolis compared to
the sleepy town of Hope.

Parking the truck, Mike turned off the engine. "I'll
take care of Katy. You just go on in."

"No!" Katy hollered from the back. "I want Nanny
Mal!"

"It'll be quicker if we all go in together," Malory
said, making a snap decision. "Okay, Katy. Uncle Mike
will unbuckle you, and you'll come in with me, okay?"

Fighting a three-year-old tended to take more time
than it was worth when out in public. She pushed open
her door and eased down to the pavement. Her center
of gravity was ever changing, it seemed. By the time
she had herself safely on the ground, Katy came running around the truck and grabbed her hand.

Mike put a hand on the small of her back, but he
kept scanning the parking lot as they walked. He still
wasn't at ease, but having him there with her did make
her feel safer. No one was getting past Mike Cruise in
one piece, that was for sure. She glanced around, wondering if she should be worried. How would she even
know? This was the first criminal ring she'd ever been
tossed into the middle of.

Mike pulled open the front door to the clinic, and Malory and Katy stepped inside in front of him. The waiting room was packed. Several pregnant women sat in one corner, small children playing with some plastic toys at their feet. A teenage girl sat next to them, looking generally unimpressed with everything around her. A few older men read magazines, and one of them looked up as Malory and Mike entered, then dropped his attention back down to his copy of *Women's Housekeeping*. As Malory approached the front desk, a scrubs-clad receptionist gave her an absent smile.

"Good morning."

"Hi, I'm Malory Smythe. I have an appointment, but I'm a little late. I'm sorry."

"Miss Smythe." The woman looked at her computer screen. "We're shorthanded today, so we're backed up. If you hurry, we can get you into a room and you won't miss your appointment."

"Oh, thank you!" Malory heaved a sigh of relief. "I really appreciate it."

"Well, children do make things more complicated, don't they?" She beamed at Katy and picked up a clipboard with a pen attached. "How old is she?"

"She's three."

"Such a great age." She came around the front of the counter. "So just come along with me. Dad, I'm going to need you, too."

The receptionist grabbed Mike by the arm and hustled them down a pink hallway interspersed with pale green doors. Katy jogged along next to Malory to keep up, her little shoes padding on the carpet. Every time Malory opened her mouth to set the receptionist straight about Mike, someone would come out a door, clipboard in hand, and they'd all get squeezed to the side.

The receptionist opened a door at the end of the hallway into a dim room and gestured them inside. The room was surprisingly large. An armchair was on one side of the room with a few magazines on its seat. Across from it, a raised bed covered in a sheet of white paper loomed next to a clunky-looking computer atop a metal cart.

"Actually—" Malory began.

"Now just get comfortable," the woman said briskly. "Dad, I'm glad you came along. I need you to help her up onto the bed. Here is a sheet. We need a bare tummy. The technologist will be here in a moment. Also, fill out this, would you?"

She thrust the clipboard into his hands, and with that, she shut the door firmly behind her, leaving them in uncomfortable silence.

So much for privacy.

MIKE LOOKED DOWN at the clipboard, then back to Malory. This had not exactly been the plan, but that receptionist had caught him by surprise, and he hadn't wanted to slow down her momentum and ruin Malory's chances of getting her ultrasound. Now he found himself in the awkward position of being assumed the father of her baby.

He handed her the clipboard. "You probably want that."

"Thanks." She sighed. "Well, if you could take Katy to the waiting room, obviously I'm safe enough in here."

Mike had to agree. His bodyguard services weren't exactly needed, and he bent down to Katy's level.

"Okay, kiddo," he said quietly. "Let's give Nanny Mal some privacy."

"What?" Katy's little face screwed up. "What's that?"

"That means we let her have some time to herself," he said. "Come with me and we'll go back to the waiting room. I saw some toys in there. I'll bet you could play with them."

Katy shook her head. "No. Don't wanna."

Mike sighed. This wasn't going to be the easy way, obviously, and he had visions of carrying a howling child back out to the waiting room.

"Come on."

"No!" Katy sidled up to Malory. "I want Nanny Mal."

Mike groaned inwardly and cast Malory an inquiring look. She was the expert here—how was he supposed to handle this? Malory, however, wasn't paying attention to his plight. Instead, she was rising up onto tiptoe and leaning back against the high bed.

"What are you doing?" he asked.

Malory stopped, color in her cheeks. "Nothing."

"Okay, so what do I do with Katy?"

Malory looked from Mike to Katy and back to Mike again. "Before you go, could you help me up?"

"Really?" Mike gave her a teasing grin. "Are you admitting you need a hand with something?"

"Oh, hush it and give me a boost," she retorted, but there was a flicker of amusement in her eyes.

Katy skipped over to the armchair and crawled up onto the seat, perfectly happy to stay with her nanny for the time being. Mike set the sheet and the clipboard on the end of the long bed. He was unsure how to lift a pregnant woman. Was he supposed to hold her waist, or would that hurt the baby? With a pregnant woman, all of her seemed somehow sacred and private, and he looked at her uncertainly.

"How is this done?" he asked.

"I have no idea," she admitted.

"Okay, I'm just going to lift you." He bent, put one hand under her knees and scooped her up into his arms. She wasn't heavy, and she let out a squeak. No other woman had felt like this in his arms. She was petite, her brown eyes wide with surprise. He caught her gaze, a smile tickling his lips. Then he gently laid her on the bed.

"That seemed like overkill," she said, gasping.

"I got you up there, didn't I?" he pointed out. "I'm nothing if not efficient."

The door opened and a young man came in, dressed in pale green scrubs. He smiled at them cordially. He was slender and blond, dark-framed glasses giving him a poetic look.

"Good morning." He dug around in a pocket and

came up with a sticker, handing it to Katy. "I'm sorry about all the rush, but we've had one of those days so far. We're down two techs." He sat down at the computer and pointed to the abandoned clipboard.

"Sir, if you could just get started on this, and I'll get started with Mom over here." He lifted Malory's shirt delicately over her milky-white belly and Mike looked away, mildly embarrassed. When he glanced in her direction again, she wasn't looking at him—she was watching the tech squeeze a coil of blue gel onto her abdomen.

Katy was quietly playing with the sticker over on the chair, and for a lack of anything better to do, he looked down at the clipboard. He couldn't possibly fill out her information for her. Except for her name. He knew that much, and he wrote it in.

"So let's get started," the technician said. "I'm just going to take a few measurements, and then we can let you two get a look at your baby."

Instead of the deep annoyance he expected to read on her features, she was trying to control a laugh. Apparently, she'd decided not to correct him.

"Should I—?" Mike jabbed a thumb toward the door.

"No." She chuckled. "Besides, I think we both know what Katy will do if you try and take her out."

He nodded in agreement, loath to take that on at the moment.

"Okay," the technician said, his tone soft and soothing. "If you just want to come in a bit closer, Dad, we'll give you a look at this baby."

Malory gave him a helpless shrug, then patted the bed beside her. Mike hesitated.

"Ticktock, Dad," the young man said. "We don't have much time, so let's make the most of it."

Mike sat, and the young man began to move the sensor over Malory's abdomen.

"Looks like baby did some moving," the technician said cheerfully. "Let's find this little one again—" After a second, he stopped. "And here we have the head…"

Mike couldn't make out much on the monitor at first, but he caught Malory's deep inhale as she looked at her baby's face for the first time. Her eyes grew misty, and he could see the love shining deep within them. She didn't even seem to remember that Mike was there as she watched the screen, the technician's voice guiding her.

"Here we have a hand—you can see the bones. It looks like a wave. Hi, Mom!"

Mike stayed silent as Malory watched. Her chest rose and fell with deep, quiet breaths, and he was struck anew with her beauty. Long lashes brushed her cheeks with each blink, and her lips parted in anticipation as the sensor moved once more, in search of tiny toes. She brushed a wisp of hair off her forehead, and her gaze flickered toward Mike.

"Isn't this amazing?" she murmured.

"Definitely." He couldn't tear his eyes from her. Her creamy skin, the scattered freckles across her nose, the love that burned deep in those expressive, soft eyes— she was amazing.

"And now is the million-dollar question." The technician turned. "Do you two want to know the gender?"

"Yes!" Malory said quickly.

"You, too, Dad?" The technician turned toward him, eyebrows raised.

"Yeah, me, too."

Malory cast him an amused smile. He hadn't meant to mislead anyone, but time was short, and he didn't want Malory to lose a single second of seeing her baby. The technician nodded and set to work once more.

"I wanted to show you…" he murmured. "Oh, this baby just decided to scoot around again. Let's see…"

Malory reached over and took his hand, and he squeezed her fingers in return. He could feel her surge of nervousness. Mike found himself holding his breath as he waited for the announcement. He knew that Malory's baby would have nothing to do with him, but he wanted for Malory to have the reassurance she needed—for the technician to announce a baby girl.

"And there it is." He beamed over at them. "Do you see?"

Mike did see—and the proof of sex was unmistakable.

"A boy…" Malory whispered.

"Congratulations." The technician looked between them with a smile. "You're having a boy."

Malory was blinking back tears and nodded slowly. She seemed to have forgotten her hand in his, and he ran his thumb over her smooth flesh, hoping that he might be able to send her some of his strength.

"I was expecting a girl," she admitted.

"It's common," the technician assured her. "You have a 50 percent chance of getting it right, and getting it wrong. But you're having a little boy, and he looks very active."

"Thank you." Malory nodded quickly. "A little boy is wonderful."

The technician took the sensor off her stomach and passed her a white towel. "I'll let you clean up the gel, and you can let yourselves out. If you'd like a screenshot from your session today, you can pay for it at reception. Congratulations, again."

The technician stopped to give Katy another sticker for being so good and closed the door behind him as he left the room. Mike looked at Malory, waiting for her to break the silence as she wiped the gel off her skin. She was about to pull her shirt back down to cover her belly when he took the towel from her. Silently, he wiped the last bit of gel that she couldn't see, then tossed the towel to the side.

"Thanks," she said softly, tugging the fabric down once more. She sat up and swung her legs over the side.

"You okay?" he asked.

She nodded. "I'll just have to adjust my expectations, I guess. I'm fine."

But her eyes told a different story.

Chapter Eleven

A boy. Malory sat in the truck, rolling this information around in her mind. She was having a boy. So this little bundle of flutters and hunger wouldn't be a Sadie or a Sophie. She'd have to rethink names.

"You sure you're okay?" Mike asked for the third time, and she sighed.

"I'm fine. It's just an adjustment."

"You really wanted a girl, huh?"

"I just don't know where I'd even start with a boy," she admitted.

"I think they both start the same way," Mike chuckled. "It's all pretty much diapers and milk."

"Funny," she said wryly. "But boys are different. They have different challenges. It's not about boyfriends pressuring them or mean girls. It's about looking tougher than you feel and standing up to the bully. It's a whole different ball game."

As soon as she'd discovered the sex of her baby, she'd had to change how to think about her unborn child. Instead of a sweet little girl rolling about inside, she had an adorable boy. And while her love for her baby was exactly the same, it was different to think about a boy than a girl. His life would look different. His toys, his friends, the games she would play with him. The realization left her slightly guilty. She'd been looking forward to tea parties and girl talks.

"You're going to need more help than you thought," Mike said, his voice low and hardly discernible past the rumble of the truck's engine.

His comment was spot-on, and that annoyed Malory more than it reassured her. He was right; she'd need more help than she'd thought. She'd need good men in her son's life to show him how it was done. She'd need advice when he was old enough to like girls and needed "the talk."

"Not everyone has an ideal situation," Malory finally said.

"I get that." He shot her an unfathomable look. "But I need help with Katy, too."

"That's different."

"Is it? Maybe a woman would have taken everything in stride, but I couldn't just drop my job, and figuring out how to care for a preschooler wasn't second nature to me. I needed help, and I did the only thing I could think of."

"Hired a nanny?"

"Pretty much."

Malory's stomach sank. She'd been so preoccupied with her own pregnancy that she'd forgotten that Mike had been thrust into parenthood, too—just three years later.

"There's nothing wrong with accepting help." She sighed. "I didn't mean this as a judgment on you."

"If it's so terrible to accept help for you, why not for me?" he countered. "What's the difference?"

"You're a man. How could you be expected to simply jump into raising a little girl and know how it's done?"

"Is it any different for a woman raising a boy?"

"It's supposed to be," she replied, then shrugged.

No one really expected a man to take to parenting instinctively, but they certainly expected a woman to be able to fill the role at a moment's notice. When a man was alone with a child, the entire community wanted to give him a hand. Men and babies—even men and toddlers—were pitied. Women, on the other hand, were supposed to have all the tools necessary to parent, and if she had to be utterly truthful with herself, raising a boy on her own scared her a lot.

"I'll figure it out," she added. "And I'll be fine."

The last part was for her. If she said it often enough, she'd believe it, and believing it was half the battle.

Katy fell asleep as they drove into Hope, and Mike and Malory remained silent, sealed away in their own thoughts. She sensed that she'd somehow disappointed him. He wanted her to need a man around. Some help sometimes? Maybe. Some advice when she was out of her depth? Perhaps. But the important things like security, stability and a safe home, she could make on her own without leaning on a man.

Mike pulled into the driveway and turned off the engine. He glanced into the backseat at the sleeping Katy.

"I'll carry her in," he said.

"I can manage," she replied.

"I want to." There was finality in his tone, and Malory didn't protest. It was a good sign that he was showing warmth toward the girl, but she couldn't help but wonder if he felt as if he had something to prove to her, too—that he could do this without her help.

She slid out of the truck and met Mike on the other side, Katy draped over his shoulder. Her little arms hung limply down, her blond curls tousled. Her feet dangled down over Mike's chest, miniature sandals turned in at the toes, and she sighed softly in her sleep.

"Hey," he said quietly.

Malory looked up at him.

"I know it wasn't really the plan today, but thanks for letting me see your baby. He's a great-looking kid."

"He is, isn't he?"

Tears glistened in her eyes, and she didn't even know why. She silently cursed the hormones and picked up her pace to open the front door—and to dry her eyes before he noticed. The door wasn't locked—a surprise, since she remembered locking it herself the last time she came out with clean clothes for Katy that morning.

When the door swung in, her stomach dropped. The house was in shambles. Furniture was tipped over, cushions had been slashed and drawers had been emptied. The large TV had a spiderweb of cracks circling out from a center of impact. She stood there, stunned, as she took in the damage.

Who would do this? Her mind spun. They weren't safe, were they? Something much bigger was at play here, and she was officially caught in the middle. She looked back toward Mike as he joined her.

"What's wrong?" he asked, but instead of any show of surprise, he put an iron grip on her arm and pulled her easily back out of the house.

"Take Katy to the truck," he ordered, bending over to slide the sleeping girl into her arms. "And lock the doors."

Pulling a gun from a holster up the back of his shirt, he went into the house.

THE HOUSE WAS empty but in tatters, and ten minutes later, Mike hopped up into the truck next to Malory and put the vehicle into gear. There wasn't much else to do at the house, and he had way more resources at his disposal at the sheriff's department.

The station was abuzz as Mike strode inside, Malory and Katy in tow. One side of the room was occupied by desks, several of which were manned by officers hunched over paperwork or on the phone. Mike's desk was in the far corner, opposite to the deputy chief's office, and he'd gotten territorial over his little corner over the years. It was a great spot—far enough from the door that he could get some work done, and far enough from the DC's office to avoid being put onto every little project that came along. His corner was nicely out of the line of sight—just the way he liked it. That was the way he liked his life, too, and the fact that he'd just had his home ransacked ticked him off on a pretty deep level.

Later on, he'd take his frustration out on a punching bag. For now he had a more immediate target in mind.

The station hummed with the cacophony of voices mingled with the rattle of an air-conditioning vent. The smell of slightly burnt coffee came from the kitchen—truth be told, that was about as good as the coffee got here.

"So they hit your place in earnest this time, did they?" Tuck asked, falling into step beside him.

"Sure did."

"You think your old man is involved?"

Mike didn't answer, and he knew that Tuck didn't need him to. Everything started when his father arrived back in town, and a place the size of Hope, Montana, didn't attract that much attention. The coincidence was a little too big to be ignored.

"How bad is it?" Tuck asked.

"It's completely torn apart."

"We'll help you get it back together," Tuck said. "You're not going to get chased out of your home."

"Thanks." Mike glanced back at Malory. Her expression was grim, and her complexion had turned paler as the morning wore on.

"She's hungry," Mike said and changed course for the kitchen. "She needs to eat something."

Pushing the kitchen door open, Mike nodded, directing her inside. "There are donuts, bagels, some cream cheese in the fridge. There should be some apples in there, too. And some truly terrible coffee. Help yourself, okay, Mal?"

She cast him a grateful smile. "Thanks. I'm getting pretty hungry."

"I thought so."

Malory and Katy went into the kitchen, and Mike headed off in the direction of the lockup. It was better that the girls not see this part anyway.

"Not going to ask for permission to question him?" Tuck asked.

"Nope." Mike shot his partner a bleak look. "You don't need to be here for this, if you don't want to be."

Tuck didn't answer but didn't peel off, either, and Mike felt a grateful swell for his reliable partner. It didn't matter what came his way, he knew he could count on Tuck.

The lockup was cut off from the rest of the station, separated by a metal door. Inside were three cells, two of which were empty. In the far cell, Nate hunkered on the edge of his bunk. He looked up as Mike came in, hope flickering in those small dark eyes.

"Hey, you came to see me," Nate said, rising to his feet. "I knew you'd come."

"Yeah?" Mike wasn't feeling like having a warm father-son moment. "I'll bet. So tell me what you know."

"I did."

"No, you didn't," Mike replied, opening the cell door.

"You letting me out?" Nate asked cautiously.

"Nope." Mike leaned against the bar and eyed his father, watching for signs of nerves. "Just here to see what you didn't tell me."

"I told you everything, son," his father said earnestly. "Everything."

"Don't pull the whole 'son' card on me," Mike replied tersely. "Why did my house get ransacked this morning?"

Genuine surprise registered on Nate's haggard face, then fear. "What are you talking about?"

"I came back to my house this morning to find it torn apart. Very efficiently done."

Nate didn't answer, and Mike let the silence stretch. The older man looked down, to the side where Tuck stood, anywhere but at Mike.

"Look…" Nate said slowly. "It isn't me, okay?"

"Obviously. You're in lockup. So who?"

"I might have mentioned that I thought I could get the money from my son's place."

"And who did you mention this to?" Mike asked, his tone low and angry.

"The guy I owe."

"Not specific enough."

"If I tell you, and you let me out of here, he'll kill me." Nate's fervent gaze moved anxiously over Mike's face. "Do you get that? Kill me."

Mike sighed. He might not like his father very much, but he did care about him. "So I'll keep it unofficial for now."

"Not good enough," Nate replied. "I'd need protection."

"That's FBI jurisdiction." Mike sighed. "Look, Dad, I'm not going to let you get killed, okay? But I need to figure out what's going on. It's not just me anymore. I have other people to take care of, too."

"Katherine." Nate's tone changed, and Mike eyed him suspiciously.

"Yes, Katherine."

Nate sighed. "Just keep me behind bars for a while, son. Deal?"

"Deal." Mike paused. There were other people who might get hurt by Nate talking, too, and he hated this part of the job—the responsibility for the outcome of whatever happened here. "What about your girlfriend? Is she in danger?"

"Gina's far away from all this. I thought I could turn it around, you know, after I got some money to impress her. She was going to be a whole new start for me." Nate shook his head. "Whatever. Look, I'll tell you who it is, but my life is in your hands now."

"Okay." Mike nodded.

"It's Sinclair Moody."

Mike paused, letting the information settle into his mind. "The thug Crystal was working for?"

"Yeah."

His cousin had been arrested on a whole cocktail of charges, from drug selling to prostitution. Sinclair Moody was the piece of work who'd strong-armed her into it, but no one could prove it. He was too slick, and he knew how to set up a fall guy.

"You were dumb enough to work with that piece of garbage?" Mike demanded. "What were you thinking?"

"Didn't know it was him. It was just a friendly poker game that turned ugly. Turned out that he was the one who kept giving me more credit. And then I lost it all and I owed more than I could pay back."

"And he offered you a deal you couldn't refuse?"

"He said I could work for him."

"And he's the one you sent after me?" Mike and Tuck exchanged a look.

"No! I swear!" Nate sighed. "I wouldn't do that. When I figured out who he was, I knew he'd do the same thing to me that he did to Crystal. I don't want jail time. Not again. So I said I'd pay him back, and he wanted to know how. I said I'd get it from you, that you had some family heirlooms that were worth a fortune."

"So Sinclair Moody thinks I have something worthwhile, does he?" Mike shook his head. "He's pretty gutsy to rob law enforcement."

"He's a bad guy, son," Nate said, his voice hopeless. "He's dangerous. An animal."

People wondered why Mike didn't trust easily, and this was the reason right here. His own father would send a seasoned criminal after him, chasing a phantom fortune—all in a split-second decision to save his own hide. The fortune didn't exist, but Sinclair Moody wouldn't be easily convinced of that.

"So you sent him in my direction. Nice."

Nate shook his head. "I was needing a drink so bad. I wasn't thinking straight. I didn't mean to."

That was something Mike could believe. When his father needed a drink, he turned into a bit of an animal.

"So if you were making up the whole thing, why on earth did you rob me?"

"I needed something—anything! You know what he'll do to me if I don't pay up."

"Yeah." Mike was absolutely clear on that little detail. Sinclair Moody had a reputation. "So how does Crystal fit into this?"

"Coincidence?" Nate shrugged.

Mike didn't believe in that much coincidence, and he had a sinking suspicion that Crystal hadn't given up Katy quite as willingly as everyone thought. He could legally have her adopted by a nice, safe family somewhere, but he'd never feel quite right about it if he didn't find the answers that made sense of this whole mess.

"All right," Mike said. "That's all for now. If you think of anything else that you failed to mention, tell one of the officers to give me a call."

"Where are you going?" Nate asked nervously.

"Don't worry," Mike said, softening his tone. "I'll make sure you stay safely locked up for the next little while."

Nate nodded. "Hey, do you think I could call Gina? I mean, she'll miss me, and—" He cleared his throat. "She's all I can think of right now."

Mike eyed his father curiously. If he wasn't mistaken, his father was in love. The idea surprised him enough to leave him skeptical. He'd never really thought of his father as capable of anything but selfish drive. If he'd loved his son at all, he'd managed to hide it pretty successfully.

"Yeah, sure."

Tuck locked the cell door, and they headed out. He

had to wonder if his father was telling the truth about Gina, or if she was just his way to get information out of the station. Either way, it would be recorded and they might learn something if Nate got sloppy.

"What's your plan?" Tuck asked when the door swung shut behind them.

"I'm heading out to Montana Women's Prison to have a chat with my cousin," he replied. "But I need you to stick really close to Malory and Katy."

"You bet." Tuck nodded. "Tell you what. Me and a couple of other officers will get your place cleaned up. I'm sure DC will authorize some round-the-clock patrols for your place, and I'll stay with them myself until you get back."

They'd be safe with Tuck—Mike knew that for certain. The sooner he got this cleared up, the sooner Katy and Malory would be safe permanently. That was top priority.

Chapter Twelve

Montana Women's Prison was located in Billings, the largest city Montana could offer up. The drive out was a long one, and no amount of radio chatter or country music seemed to be enough to clear Mike's thoughts as the minutes crawled by. His mind was spinning, and try as he might, he couldn't pull his thoughts away from Malory and Katy.

The miles clicked past on his odometer, the fields of young wheat melding into pasture, black-and-white cows dotting the rolling hills. A summer storm crept slowly in his direction from the west, a smudge of gray clouds that brushed the land with rain, growing ever bigger and closer.

Getting attached to Malory and Katy was downright stupid, but that didn't seem to be stopping him right now. This entire situation was complicated and messy, leaving him feeling empty, an ache inside his chest. And he couldn't really explain why. True, his house was now full of laughter and life—something he'd never experienced before in his lifetime. As a boy, he'd lived with an alcoholic father, and the experience had left him with dark, angry memories. He'd spent many an evening watching late-night TV while his father slept off his latest drinking binge on the kitchen floor. Once he lived on his own, he'd been cautious, protecting his privacy and order—neither of which he'd had as a kid—like a miser.

He liked to keep his life orderly, but Katy's arrival had sent that order for a spin. From messy meals to laughter and play, she filled her waking hours with noise and personality. Even her tantrums didn't bother him as much as he'd thought they would. She was three—these things happened, right? He was growing attached, looking forward to seeing her bright smile and checking on her at night before he went to bed. He couldn't seem to sleep unless he'd stopped at her door and looked at her. The one night he tried to skip it, he'd lain awake until he got up again, wrapped his robe around him and peered in at her sleeping form.

Safe. He had to know that she was safe.

These feelings that spun around inside him could be pushed down only so far, and the minute he stopped that downward pressure, they inched back up again. He'd never been a guy who talked about his feelings too easily, much to the complaints of past girlfriends. But he did have feelings. He just didn't like opening the lid on that mess. Some things were best kept covered.

The storm finally reached the road, huge raindrops pelting his windshield. The wipers whipped back and forth, and all he could see around him was the gray of cloud and the green of grass, flattened by pounding rain. He pulled out and passed a slower vehicle, then eased back into the lane. A semi truck lumbered by in the opposite direction, splashing his truck with muddy water.

The storm wouldn't last long. Summer storms were transitory affairs that engulfed a man completely in driving rain and cracking lightning, then passed on without a backward glance. Everything would be sun and sparkling water droplets in a matter of minutes. That was something you could count on in Montana.

By the time he arrived at the prison and parked, he hadn't sorted out any of his feelings, but he had managed to shove them all back down in order to clear his head. If nothing else, he could figure out what was going on with Sinclair Moody, and that would have to do. At least a mystery could be solved.

The visiting room was a dismal cinder-block area with a table in the center topped by a plastic tablecloth in an attempt to make it more friendly. Being a police officer, he was able to talk to his cousin without a piece of glass between them, and he found himself nervous as he waited for her to be brought in. He hadn't seen her in years, and this sort of introduction after that length of time wasn't exactly easy for either of them.

When Crystal arrived wearing an orange jump-suit, her hair pulled back into a scraggly ponytail, she stopped at the door uncertainly. She was thin—too thin—and there were rings under her eyes. She watched him, waiting.

"Hi," Mike said. "It's been a while."

Did she even know who he was? He wouldn't have recognized her without some prodding, either.

"That you, Mike?" she asked incredulously. "I haven't seen you since Grandma's house."

"It's been a few years," he admitted. "How are you doing?"

She spread her arms and laughed. She'd lost a few teeth, and her skin was pockmarked from addiction. "How do I look?"

Mike didn't know how to answer that. Instead, he gestured to the table. "We don't have a lot of time. Let's have a seat."

"What do you want?" she asked cautiously as she sat in the plastic chair. She fiddled with her thumbnail, refusing to make eye contact.

"Did you know that Katy is with me right now?" he asked.

"It's Katherine."

"Sorry. I know. We shortened it and she seems to like it."

She shrugged. "Okay. How is she?"

"She's doing great." He cleared his throat. "You signed all the papers to give away all legal rights."

"Yeah." She turned her attention to a different nail, scratching at a break.

"Why?"

"Why?" She laughed bitterly. "Do you see where I am? What can I do for her in here? What did I do for her out there, for that matter?"

"Were you pressured in any way?" Mike asked.

"Like by Social Services?" she asked.

"No, like by Sinclair Moody."

Her eyes widened at the name, then narrowed. "Why do you mention him?"

"You were working for him when you were arrested, right?"

"No one could prove that."

"Yeah, I know that no one could prove it," he retorted. "They tried. They always try. This isn't an entirely official visit. I just want to hear it from you."

"They never believed me."

"Yeah, well, I'm family. I will." The words sounded hollow on his tongue. Since when did Cruises trust each other? If anyone should know better, it would be a Cruise.

"Okay, well, I was working for him. He told us to rob that store, and I ended up killing that security guard. I didn't mean to. It just sort of happened and I found out later he had a family and all that—" She heaved a sigh. "And I went down for it. End of story."

"I have a feeling Sinclair Moody just ransacked my house."

Crystal's mouth slackened in shock, and she blinked several times, then swallowed hard. "He's after you now?"

"I have no idea what he's after, but I find the coincidence a little too large for comfort."

"It's not you," she whispered, leaning closer. "It's Katherine. He wants Katherine!"

"What makes you say that?" Mike snapped. "What does he want with a little girl?"

"Sinclair Moody is her father."

Mike stared at his cousin, the information slowly

sinking in. It made sense. If Crystal had been Sinclair's girlfriend, it would explain how he'd managed to pull her into his crime ring so quickly. She'd always been around drug addicts and criminals, so another thug was no difference. If he'd fathered a child, then let his girlfriend be the fall guy for a botched robbery, he might want the child back.

"You didn't ever put that on her papers, though," Mike said. "You said the father was unknown."

"I'm not stupid," she snapped. "But, Mike, you have to keep him away from her. He's a monster!"

"Yeah, I know." He sighed. "How far away do you want her?"

"How far can you get her?" she asked, blinking back tears.

"I want to have her adopted by another family out of state. It would be a closed adoption until she's eighteen, and that would give her fifteen years with another family to put her life together before she found out where she came from. She'd be as far from Sinclair as we could get her."

Crystal nodded. "Do it."

"We wouldn't see her again, Crystal."

"Do I look like the kind of mother she needs?" Crystal asked, shaking her head. "I'm in prison for second-degree murder. I'm a mess. All I want is some meth, and I can't get it in here, not without more money than I've got. They detoxed me, but I still want it. I've got to get myself together, and letting her know that this is her mother—" she gestured toward her jumpsuit "—isn't good for her. Let her have a better start." She grabbed Mike's sleeve in a scratching grip. "Can you get me anything? Just to get me through. Just to take the edge off…"

"Crystal, I'm a sheriff!" He pulled his arm free. "No, I can't get you any drugs."

She sank back into the chair, hunching forward. "You turned out good, Mike." Tears filled her eyes. "Don't know how you got away from this cursed family, but you turned out good."

It didn't matter how much he loved Katy or how hard it would be to give her to another dad to raise, he had to protect her. Sinclair Moody had probably figured out where his daughter was and he was coming for her. The safest place for Katy was as far away from the Cruise clan as possible. His first instincts had been right on target.

"Time's up," a guard said, opening the door, and Mike rose to his feet.

"You get her away from him!" Crystal called after him as the guard ushered him out of the room. "You hear me? Anything happens to her, and I'll kill you myself!"

Mike didn't doubt it for a minute.

MALORY WAS AMAZED at the number of people who arrived to help clean up the house that afternoon. Young couples, older people, even some teenagers, came by with cleaning supplies and toolboxes, then set to work with cheerful chatter. Katy was thrilled to have so much company, and Malory was run off her feet trying to keep her a safe distance from power tools and chemicals. However, in a matter of hours, the house was put back together, as close to normal as possible. By the time everyone left to go get a beer at the local pub, the only things remaining that revealed what had happened were some irreparable shelves that leaned against the outside of the house and the vacant spot on the wall that used to hold a television.

"I can't believe how quickly everyone cleaned this up," Malory said.

Tuck shrugged and stroked his hand over his bristly mustache. "He's done the same for us. That's what you do. You help each other. How else are folks supposed to get through?"

Malory sucked in a breath and rubbed a hand across her belly. For the past few minutes, she'd been feeling twinges, and they were getting more painful. Tuck frowned and looked her over.

"You okay?" he asked.

"I think so. Just a bit sore."

"You'd better sit," he said.

Malory didn't need any more coaxing. She moved over to the couch and eased down onto a cushion. She sucked in again as one of the twinges turned more insistent. Katy came into the living room from the kitchen, her bear clutched in her arms, and she froze, her big blue eyes fixed on her nanny.

"Do you need a doctor?" Tuck asked.

Malory shook her head. "Let's see if resting helps at all first."

Tuck nodded but didn't look completely convinced. He set about getting her a hot cup of mint tea, and by the time he returned with it, the pain was already subsiding. Katy crawled up onto the couch next to Malory and snuggled close, her bear still clasped in her hands. Malory smoothed some blond curls away from Katy's eyes.

"Thanks for staying with us today," Malory said. "You don't even know us, but you've been so kind."

"Hey, I know Mike well enough," Tuck replied, batting aside her thanks with some discomfort. "Not that I wouldn't help otherwise. My wife and I have four kids, so I understand this part of things. It's not easy."

"No," she agreed, closing her eyes. "It's not."

She hated admitting how difficult this was right now. Those pains had scared her, and now that they were back to being twinges again, she fully intended to keep them at bay. If she could. The hardest part about pregnancy was how little control she seemed to have over her body.

"So you must know Mike pretty well," Malory said, opening her eyes.

"I've known him since high school," Tuck replied. "So yeah, better than most. He's a solid guy."

"He's been telling me a little bit about his childhood."

Tuck's eyebrows went up. "Has he, now? You should feel special, then, because he's not much of a talker."

"What do you mean?" she asked.

"It was bad back then. His dad was a mess. Drinking and fighting, getting into trouble. My parents hated me spending time with Mike because of his father, but it wasn't Mike's fault. The best thing that ever happened was his old man walking out on him and leaving him by himself. It was easier for Mike alone. When his dad was there, Mike had to take care of both of them. Without his father, he only had to take care of himself."

"And he doesn't talk about it?" Malory asked.

Tuck shook his head. "He likes to leave it in the past. That was a hard time. Bad memories." Tuck leaned back in the chair. Then a smile quirked his lips. "Actually, I can't begin to tell you how many women have complained to me that he just won't open up. And what could I tell them? That's Mike."

Malory was silent. She didn't find Mike reticent. He had told her quite a bit about his childhood and his difficulties with his father. For some reason, he seemed to trust her, and that left a warm glow inside her at the realization. She looked down at Katy, whose eyes were drooping with fatigue. She brushed a fingertip down Katy's nose and her lids blinked shut.

"Everyone seems to really love Mike," she said.

"He's a solid guy and a good officer. I've known him to sit on a stoop with a raging veteran until he calmed down, instead of just hauling him into the station. He's the guy who shovels an elderly neighbor's driveway in winter or takes some time with a troubled teen he picks up for shoplifting. He's helped every one of us some way or other."

"What about you?" Malory asked.

"He introduced me to my wife," Tuck replied with a grin. "Never can repay a debt that big!"

Malory chuckled. "You seem very happily married."

"You bet."

She felt a rush of movement from within, and she was relieved. The baby was still active—that was a good sign, right? And the twinges had stopped altogether now. Tuck's cell phone rang and he took the call.

"Hey, sweetheart…yeah, yeah…"

Malory snuggled Katy closer. After the past couple of days, she didn't feel comfortable carrying her upstairs to sleep just yet. While things felt a lot safer now that the house was back in order, she still couldn't put aside her fear. The state of affairs had left her and the little girl in need of protection. Katy required more than a grown-up to look out for her. She needed a parent—someone to love her absolutely and to protect her for a lifetime. Sometimes, when she thought about Katy going off to a different home, she wished she could be her mom and give her the love that she craved. But she couldn't. Malory wouldn't be in a position to adopt as a single mother already struggling.

Tuck switched the phone to his other ear. "Okay, put the phone down beside him." There was a pause. "Hey, buddy." His tone grew gentle. "You having trouble sleeping?"

Malory smiled wistfully, listening to the one-sided fatherly conversation with a small boy who couldn't go to sleep. Tuck was a good dad, and his kids were lucky to have him. Her own son would probably never know his father.

After Tuck hung up the phone, he shrugged bashfully.

"That's Nicholas. He's like me, can't sleep at night."

"Do you talk to him every night when you work?" she asked.

"I'm always talking to one of them. Four kids keep you hopping."

"I can only imagine." She smiled.

"My wife stays home with the kids, but she can't do it all. Sometimes it just takes a dad's touch, you know?"

Malory nodded, and Tuck grimaced.

"Look, I'm sorry. I know you've got a special situation and all—"

"No, it's fine," she replied. "You're a good father and you shouldn't apologize for that. I'll have a support network of my own, so no need to worry."

Tuck nodded. He rose to his feet and looked at his watch. "I'm just going to take a quick look around the perimeter."

Lying on the couch, Katy snuggled up in her arms, Malory realized that she missed Mike. Mike was more than police protection—he was comforting in a different way. He seemed like a part of this scene somehow, and snuggling up with Katy just wasn't complete without him.

Is this what a family feels like?

She hardly dared to imagine it. Now was not the time to let herself get sentimental about something that wasn't hers. It didn't matter if she was falling for the big sheriff or not—it wasn't realistic. It was better to embrace the family that she did have—the people who were rightfully hers. She would move back to her mother's house in time to have the baby. Her son needed to come first.

She pulled out her cell phone and dialed her mother's number. It rang twice before her mom picked up.

"How are you doing over there?" her mother asked.

How was she doing? She was in an emotional upheaval, her body was warning her to rest and she found herself missing the man she wasn't supposed to be falling in love with. But she didn't want to talk about those things, because they scared her the most. So instead, she said, "The house was broken into again."

"And you immediately quit and bought a ticket home, right?"

"No," Malory said. "I'm surrounded by deputies. Couldn't be safer, I promise."

If her mother could see Mike, with his broad shoulders and solid muscles, she'd stop worrying immediately. Malory wasn't in danger from a thug—not with Mike looking out for her.

"Why don't you just come back?" her mother insisted. Then there was a muffled voice in the background. "Ted agrees with me. He says he can have your room in order by tonight. Just get on a plane already."

"No, no, I've got a job to do," Malory replied. "And I need the health insurance, remember? Mike has it all under control."

"Are you sure you're safe?" her mother pressed.

She was safer here under the watchful eyes of the Hope Sheriff's Department. If she walked away, who was to say what would happen to her? Something big was at work here, and she felt like a rabbit in the bush with a hawk circling overhead. Sometimes just hunkering low was the best option.

"I wouldn't put my baby in danger, Mom. You can trust this."

"Okay." She was quiet for a moment. "Wait—weren't you supposed to have your ultrasound today? Did you miss it?"

"No, I went."

"And?" her mother prodded. "Did you find out?"

"It's a boy."

"A boy! That's wonderful. A little boy… It'll be fun. Now I know what color to buy—just hold me back at Walmart."

"No room for error." Malory closed her eyes. "But my instincts were off."

"They will be."

"What?" She opened her eyes.

Her mother chuckled. "Don't tell your son until he's grown-up with kids of his own, but of course you'll get it wrong sometimes. All you can do is your best. Loving him will make up the difference."

"Will it be enough, Mom?"

"It was for you. And I made plenty of mistakes," her mother admitted. "Do you remember when I let you eat all your Halloween candy in one night and you spent the next day throwing up?"

"You told me you were letting me learn a lesson," Malory said.

"That was a lie. I didn't know it would make you sick."

Malory laughed. "But I don't know how to raise a boy, Mom."

"I didn't know how to raise a girl," her mother pointed out. "I had little brothers, remember? We sorted it out together, you and I."

"And never had a proper bedtime," Malory said, "if I remember properly."

"See? And you turned out fine."

Her mother had done a good job with her, in spite of her mistakes. If Malory could just avoid her mother's biggest error in judgment when it came to dating, she might be able to do this after all.

"You know, Malory, my neighbor has a single son—"

"Mom, no." Malory shook her head. "That's where I draw the line. Just leave my love life to me."

"Oh." Her mother sighed. "Maybe it's just the hormones right now. After the baby's born, there's no reason why you can't get back out there and meet someone. You're so cautious when it comes to men. You don't bounce back very easily…"

It wasn't the hormones, but her mother was right—she didn't bounce back and she didn't expect her child to, either. She'd be a mother—100 percent—and she'd never make her son feel like second fiddle to some boyfriend passing through their lives. She'd do things differently than her mother had, and with any luck, her son would grow up without too many complaints. Would she be so lucky?

After a little more chitchat about her mother's upcoming wedding plans, she said good-night and hung up.

This was the family she had, and this was the family she should cherish. The last thing she needed to do right now was to court unnecessary heartbreak.

Chapter Thirteen

The next morning, Mike stood in front of his house, scanning the yard. A squad car cruised past and flashed the lights at him in greeting, but besides the presence of law enforcement, the place seemed quiet. All he'd been thinking about for the entire long drive home was finding Malory to talk this whole thing out, but when he got back, she was asleep on the couch. After Tuck left, Mike hadn't had the heart to wake her, so he locked up and carried Katy up to bed. Malory and Katy were both asleep still, even though it was nearly nine o'clock. The past few days had drained them, it seemed, and he felt an obligation to protect their rest.

Don't get used to this.

He knew better than to start relying on Malory as the woman in his life. He knew that he was already blurring the lines with her, and that was dangerous territory. She was his responsibility, but he wasn't hers. That was the difference. It was his duty to protect her, but she owed him nothing more than the services of a nanny.

The breeze was cool and laden with the scent of lilacs. It was the kind of summer morning he usually enjoyed, sitting on his steps and looking up into that vast night sky. Today his mind was on his own responsibilities, and no amount of staring at the horizon was going to change what they were.

His cell phone vibrated in his pocket. Checking it, he recognized the number from the adoption agency, and his heart sank. This was it.

Picking up the call, Mike sat down on the steps.

"This is Mike Cruise."

"Hello, Mr. Cruise, this is Elizabeth Nelson from the adoption agency. How are you this morning?"

"Good," he replied, keeping his voice low. "How are you?"

"I'm well. We have a family who is very interested in meeting Katy. They are Ned and Belinda Petersen, a doctor and a stay-at-home mom. They have two other children in high school, and when they saw the picture of Katy, they just melted."

This was the news he'd been waiting for, but it didn't make him feel the relief he thought he'd feel.

"That's…uh…great." He cleared his throat. "Where do they live?"

"Wyoming. Is that a problem?"

"No, that's actually perfect." Out of state. Exactly what they needed.

"They'd love to meet her, but there's a hitch. They'll be in the area tomorrow. Is that too soon for you?"

"No, that should be fine," Mike replied, his tone wooden. "What time should we expect them?"

"About nine in the morning," Ms. Nelson said.

"Thank you, Mr. Cruise. I don't want to make any promises, but I have a good feeling about this match."

After hanging up, he stared at the face of the touch screen. So this was it—and if it wasn't this family, it would be another one. Someone would come along and fall in love with that bright-eyed little girl and take her home to raise her.

He knew it was for the best. Katy needed safety and security. She needed to be away from the Cruises, and this was her chance at freedom. Yet for some reason, he still hesitated. This was exactly what she needed, but he didn't want to let all of this go. His life had turned upside down with her arrival, and instead of being relieved at being able to go back to his familiar bachelor life, he felt an ache deep inside.

He'd never see her again, if this worked according to plan—not that she'd know of, at least. He'd keep an eye on her from a distance, but she'd likely forget him completely—a foggy memory if anything. And when Katy left, so would Malory. That hit him in that tender place, too. They weren't his family, but a part of him was starting to see them that way.

With a sigh, Mike pushed himself to his feet. Maybe it was time to start thinking more seriously about getting that family of his own instead of getting attached to the people who wouldn't stay. He was setting himself up for heartbreak, plain and simple.

"Pull it together, man," he muttered to himself and opened the door.

Malory lay on the couch, snoring softly. Her hair fell away from her face, exposing her creamy neck.

Her breathing hitched and she shifted slightly, her hand smoothing over her belly. She hadn't woken. As he watched her, tenderness squeezed his heart.

A clock ticked away in the hall in time to the soft breathing coming from the couch. She was beautiful in her slumber, and he wondered what it might be like to have a wife of his own, just like Malory.

It was too easy to imagine, and he shut it down. One day he'd build that family of his own, but right now he had other priorities—namely keeping these two safe.

MALORY'S EYES FLUTTERED open at the sound of Mike's familiar tread in the kitchen. It took her a moment to orient herself, and she yawned. Tuck was gone, as was Katy, and she sat up, looking around. The sun was up, and the house was dim, the curtains blocking most of the morning light.

"Good morning," Mike said as he appeared in the kitchen doorway and saw her awake. "Sleep well?"

Malory nodded and stifled another yawn. "I thought I was resting my eyes until you got home."

Mike chuckled. "You were out cold. I didn't have the heart to disturb you."

"So how did it go?" she asked.

Mike considered. "Let's hear about your day first."

Malory swung her legs over to sit properly on the couch. She ran a hand over her stomach, and the baby fluttered in response.

"I think I overdid it a little bit," she admitted.

"What do you mean?" Mike's brow furrowed, and

he came over to the couch and sank down next to her. "Are you okay?"

"I'm fine now." She wasn't sure why she wanted to reassure him so badly. "But I was having some twinges."

"That's not good." He looked down at her, concern in his dark eyes. "I can take over more with Katy so you can get some rest."

Why did he have to be so kind? Sometimes she wished he'd just be more professionally distant and ask her if she wanted a few hours of unpaid leave or something.

"That's not how it's supposed to be when you hire a nanny," she said quietly. "You brought me in for full-time child care. If I can't provide that, maybe it's better to—"

"Find someone else? No." He shrugged. "If I were her father, she'd need time with me, too. So let's just say I'll do more with Katy, and it should balance out."

"True." She frowned slightly. "Are you thinking about keeping her?"

Mike didn't answer for a moment, his emotions hidden behind that granite mask. Then he cleared his throat. "No. I'm not."

"What's going on?" Malory asked quietly.

"Tomorrow morning a couple is coming to meet Katy. They're interested in adoption."

Malory blinked, took a deep breath. "So soon?"

"They're going to be in the area tomorrow," Mike said. "The adoption agency asked if a visit would be possible."

Malory didn't say anything, but her heart was heavy. She had grown attached to the little girl over the past couple of weeks, and while she'd known that this was the plan from the very beginning, the news still hurt.

"How do you feel about it?" Malory asked.

"Me?" Mike shook his head. "Does it matter?"

"To me," she replied.

Mike's smile was sad, his reserve cracking ever so slightly. Sucking in a deep breath, he shrugged. "I got more attached than I thought."

"Me, too," she admitted. "She's such a special little girl."

"And smart, too." He nodded. "I'm going to miss her."

Malory eyed him speculatively. "Then why let her go? You have a choice, don't you? If you wanted to keep her and raise her yourself, you could."

He scrubbed a hand through his hair, then leaned forward, resting his elbows on his knees. "I wasn't going to tell you this." His tone was gravelly, and for a long moment, he didn't say anything else, making her wonder if perhaps he'd reconsidered telling her anything at all.

"What is it?" she prompted.

"I went to see my cousin in prison, Crystal—Katy's mom."

"Oh?" She was breathless in spite of herself. "What did she say?"

"Among other things, that Katy is the result of Crystal's romantic relationship with a very dangerous man." He turned his head to look at her. "Really dangerous."

"Can you tell me who?" she asked cautiously.

"I shouldn't," he replied quietly. "It's for your own safety. Suffice it to say that he's someone who has done some pretty nasty stuff, but even the FBI can't seem to nail him down."

A shiver ran up Malory's back. There was something in Mike's eyes that told her this was no exaggeration. As his words sank in, another thought occurred to her. How safe were they, exactly?

"Is this the same guy who broke into the house?" Malory asked.

"I think so." He nodded. "Of course, it can't be proven, but the coincidences are a little too strong for my liking. That's how these guys get so powerful. They stay one step ahead of the law and make sure that everyone is so scared of them they'll never testify. A middling lawyer and no testimony in court is all a scumbag needs to get off free."

"Do you think he's coming after Katy?"

"Let's put it this way," Mike said quietly. "If he wasn't coming after her before, he knows she's here now, and he certainly wouldn't be opposed to using her for his own gain."

Malory shuddered. "But how did he find her?"

"My father." The words were low and bitter.

"Oh." She shook her head slowly. "So how safe are we right now?"

"You?" He shot her a grim smile. "You're safe with me, babe. You can count on that."

She smiled at the determination in his voice. If there

was one place she felt safe right now, it was next to this big sheriff.

"And when Katy is settled with a new family," she clarified. "Will it be dangerous for me to go home? Is anyone going to be following me, too?"

Mike paused again, and she thought she detected sadness in those dark eyes. "No, you'll be able to go home. I'll talk it over with the chief, but my instincts say that this guy is after me and Katy—not you."

Malory didn't feel any relief at those words. The fact that this criminal was after Mike and Katy kept the stakes just as high. What would he do if he caught up to them?

"That doesn't make me feel a whole lot better," she admitted, tears misting her eyes.

He smiled and reached over, putting a broad palm against her cheek. "I've got it under control."

"Do you really?" she asked. "Because if anything happened to you—"

"You'd start drinking?" he asked, a teasing glint in his eye. He didn't take his hand away from her face, and she leaned in to his touch. Malory's heavy sadness didn't lift, a solid mass holding her down.

"It wouldn't be pretty," she said.

"Nothing's going to happen to us." He ran his fingers through her hair. "And Katy is going to go where she'll be safe—and out of reach." He dropped his hand and leaned back down, resting his elbows on his knees. "This whole Cruise family is rotten to the core."

"No, it isn't," she replied, leaning forward and slipping her hand around his warm, solid biceps.

"You haven't met us," he said wryly.

"I've met you."

He looked away, eyes glistening.

"You're a good man, Mike Cruise. A good man, and a lot of people are lucky to have you looking out for them."

Mike turned toward her, and with a tickle of surprise, she found his face inches from hers. Her breath caught, but she didn't pull back. He was warm, sturdy, emanating heat against her, and in that room with only this one rugged man between her and a ruthless criminal, she felt utterly safe. His dark eyes moved slowly over her face, and he smiled wistfully down at her. He didn't say anything—didn't have to. He leaned closer, his breath whispering against her skin, then closed the gap between them as his warm lips met hers.

Malory leaned into his shoulder, and he turned, slipping an arm around her waist, tugging her closer still. He was strong as iron, but he responded to her as she pulled back, putting a hand against his chest to give herself some breathing room, only to feel the insistent rhythm of his heart.

"I don't think I'm thinking straight," she murmured.

Mike released her. "Sorry. I probably shouldn't have done that."

She shrugged and laughed softly. "No, I just need to—" She didn't know what she needed to do. She needed to think. She needed to get her head back together. She needed to get far enough away from those smoldering eyes that she could remember why this was such a bad idea.

The baby gave her a soft kick, and she breathed in, putting her hand against her belly.

That was why. She rose to her feet.

"I'd better go check on Katy, Mike."

He nodded. "You okay?"

"I'm fine." She felt the heat in her cheeks. "But— Mike, I'm going home to my mother to have my baby."

"Oh…" He blinked. "Okay, I guess that's understandable."

"I know I promised to stay as long as you needed me, but I have to think about my son, now, and…"

"No, I get it." His voice was deep and quiet. "I'm going to miss you, Nanny Mal."

She headed up the stairs, her heart still pounding from that kiss. She looked back to see the big man sitting right where she'd left him, elbows on his knees and head hanging down as if he shouldered the weight of more than she'd ever know.

Chapter Fourteen

The next morning, Mike stood in the kitchen alone, listening to the sound of Katy giggling on the second floor. He leaned against the counter, a mug of hot coffee in one hand, waiting. The Petersens would arrive any minute now, and the ball would start rolling.

Unless they didn't bond with Katy somehow.

Was he hoping? Part of him was, but he couldn't push aside reality. Katy's father was a criminal, and her safety meant more than Mike's attachment to her. The child who, when he'd first heard of her, had seemed like an unnerving responsibility had taken over a bigger part of his heart than he'd thought possible. The Cruise family had always felt like a curse, and he'd distanced himself from them. The fact that Katy was a Cruise, however, made her just a little more dear to him. She was a girl who not only shared his bloodline but had a chance at a life free of her family's stigma.

There was a thump and another eruption of giggles, calmed by Malory's soothing tones. He smiled to himself. Somehow, this fantasy of family life had grown for him, and it included Malory. When Katy left, so would her nanny, and Malory wasn't just the nanny to him anymore, either.

Not that she wants this, he reminded himself firmly. He'd kissed her the day before, and she'd kissed him back. But then she'd pulled away and headed upstairs to her own personal space. But this time he didn't kick himself. It hadn't been a mistake. He'd kissed her, and he'd meant it—whatever that kiss had meant. For once, he wasn't sorry.

There was a knock on the door, and he set his coffee down on the counter. He took a deep breath, then headed out through the living room to the front door. Opening it, he was met with a slim, well-kempt couple. The man was tall and prematurely gray and wore a polo shirt and khaki pants. His wife had chin-length blond hair and large doe-like eyes and was as slender as her husband. They smiled nervously.

"Good morning," Mike said. "You're the Petersens, I take it?"

"I'm Ned, and this is Belinda," the man said with a nod. "It's good to meet you."

They shook hands and Mike stepped back to allow them entrance. They looked around themselves briefly. Then their gazes came back to Mike.

"Come on in," Mike said, gesturing them to the couch. "Malory—the nanny—is getting Katy dressed, so they'll be down soon."

"Maybe you could tell us a little about Katy," Belinda said, sitting down next to her husband in the center of the couch. "What sorts of things does she like to do?"

The couple looked at him expectantly, and sitting there together on the couch, he realized that they were both wearing the exact same shade of khaki pants.

"Well, she's a smart kid who is really full of energy," he said. "She needs a challenge, or else she gets bored. For example, Malory has been teaching her the alphabet, and she knows almost all her letters now, and she's only been here two weeks."

"Wow," Ned said with a smile. "That's really good. How old is she?"

"Three."

"She sounds very intelligent," Ned said. "We'd be able to place her with a top preschool. A Montessori school might be a great match for her abilities."

"She's had a tough start, though," Mike went on. "She's a sweet girl with a big heart, and her world hasn't made a whole lot of sense to her so far. She needs a lot of love."

"The mother—" Belinda winced. "She wouldn't want... I mean, is she—?"

"No, the adoption would be a closed one." Mike saved her from the awkward question. "The mother wants what's best for Katy, and she knows that she can't provide the kind of home her daughter needs."

Belinda breathed out a sigh of relief. "Oh, that's good. Hopefully, she won't remember any of that, since she's so young."

Mike could understand the sentiment, but did he really want her to forget everything? She was a Cruise, after all, and while her mother was an addict who'd made some horrible blunders, Crystal still wanted what was best for Katy in the end. Did she deserve to be erased? Did Mike want Katy to forget about him, as well?

"Even if she doesn't remember it, it's going to be a part of her," Mike countered. "She's going to need understanding, someone who can help her to learn a new way of seeing the world."

"Of course, of course," Ned said quickly. "We can get her the top therapists. In fact, if we start her early, she could have a pediatric therapist for as many years as she needs. Our financial resources aren't a problem, I can assure you. I'm a pediatrician myself, so I'd be able to find her the best support possible."

Mike nodded. They were almost too perfect, this slim, khaki-clad couple, but they had everything to offer a little girl, and she'd grow up with the best of everything from therapy to a pony, no doubt. He heard footsteps coming down the stairs, and the couple turned to see the little girl in her pink dress. Malory came behind, and she smiled at the couple. Then her gaze moved to Mike. This was hard for her, too—he could see it in her eyes.

"Katy, these are our friends Mr. and Mrs. Petersen," Mike said. "Why don't you come say hi?"

Katy skipped over, sidling up to Mike and leaning against his leg. She didn't say anything to the couple but looked at them speculatively.

"We brought you a present," Belinda said. "Would you like to see it?"

"A present?" Katy's eyes lit up. "For me?"

Belinda pulled out a gift bag and held out her arms for Katy. "Do you want to come see it with me?"

Katy hesitated, then scooted around Ned and closer to Belinda, peering curiously down into the bag. As Katy pulled out a baby doll, her face bright with excitement, Mike rose to his feet and joined Malory near the doorway. Her arms were crossed over her chest, and she was blinking away tears as she watched the Petersens interacting with the little girl.

"What do you think?" Mike whispered.

"They seem nice," she murmured back.

"He's a pediatrician. They're already talking about Montessori schools and getting her the best therapists to help her adjust."

Malory glanced up at him. "They've got a lot to offer."

Mike nodded but didn't answer. They did have a lot to offer her, he couldn't argue with that, but something inside him hesitated. Malory rested her hand on her belly and while she didn't flinch, it was obvious that she was uncomfortable.

"You okay?" he asked.

She nodded. "Those twinges. I think I'm just a little upset. I know this is good for Katy, but it's still hard."

"Yeah." Mike nodded. "It is."

She met his gaze and gave him a sympathetic smile. He'd miss this. Malory hadn't been in his life long, but he was already finding himself relying on that smile of hers.

"She loves the doll." Malory nodded in their direction. "That was a good choice."

"A doll for a girl—that didn't take a lot of imagination," he quipped.

She shot him a wry smile. "You don't like them, do you?"

He sighed. "They're fine. What can I say?"

She smiled again, and squeezed his arm. Maybe he wouldn't have to say it aloud—that he hated how perfect they were, that he hated that they'd take over and Katy would go off to forget about her biological family.

That's a good thing, he reminded himself. *This is what she needs in order to be safe.*

Belinda reached for her purse and dug around for a moment. "Can we take a picture of us together?" she asked, pulling out a digital camera.

"Sure." Mike crossed the room and took the camera, and Belinda and Ned crouched down next to Katy, their smiles hopeful.

Mike snapped the photo, and he had to admit that they looked good together. Katy's blond hair matched Belinda's, and Katy stood proudly, her doll clutched in her arms. This just might be Katy's very first family photo in her young lifetime.

A COUPLE OF hours later, Katy munched on a peanut-butter sandwich in the kitchen, her new doll set up carefully next to her, the plastic face smeared with the peanut butter Katy was trying to feed her. Katy took a bite, chewing contentedly.

"That was actually a really good visit," Mike said quietly. "Katy seems to like them."

Malory nodded. "They were nice. What did they say when they left?"

"That they'd be in touch with the adoption agency this afternoon." He sighed. "I know this is going to sound nuts, but I'm not 100 percent sure about them."

"Why not?" Obviously, Mike had been noticing different things than she had. She'd seen a well-dressed couple who were educated and willing to pour both their love and their resources into a child. Was there something sinister lurking beneath that she hadn't sensed?

"Ned's a bit of a—" he cast around for the word "—dweeb."

"Dweeb?" Malory laughed aloud and shook her head. "I thought this was going to be some sort of sheriff's instinct."

"Who says it isn't?" He chuckled. "Plus, their pants matched."

"It was cute," she countered.

"I'll bet they jog in matching fuchsia tracksuits." He grinned. "And his teeth are impossibly white."

"That's all you've got?" she asked, smothering a laugh.

"Yeah, that's it," he admitted.

Malory rubbed her stomach, the twinges she'd been feeling earlier back again and this time more insistent. She breathed deeply.

"They kind of looked alike," Mike said. "Are couples supposed to look alike? They were almost like brother and sister."

"I've heard people start to look alike over time—"

She stopped and sucked in another breath as a twinge grew more painful. "Oh...that one hurt."

"What's happening?" Mike asked, the jokiness dropping from his tone. "You don't look good."

"Those pains—" She pressed her lips together against the pain and leaned over against the counter.

"Okay, you're going to sit down," Mike said, putting his arm around her and guiding her toward a chair. "Come on—" He hooked a chair leg with one foot and pulled it the rest of the way to meet her.

"I don't think I need—" She didn't finish the sentence, because the tightening was so strong it was too painful to talk through.

"Yeah, you do," Mike replied.

"I'll just rest a bit," she said, as the tightening passed.

"Good idea." Mike eyed her cautiously. "You sure you're okay?"

"I'm fine, I'm fine." She ignored his concern. "Don't you want to know what I thought of them?"

"Actually, I do," he said, leaning against the counter. "You're pretty intuitive."

"I think that they are the type of people that you'd never be friends with," she said with a shrug. "You'd never sit down and have some wings with Ned. He'd never go jogging with you in his pink tracksuit."

"Fuchsia."

"Fine, his fuchsia tracksuit." She laughed and shook her head. "And that's fine. They don't have to be the kind of people you'd bond with in order to be good and devoted parents."

"You're being very mature about this," Mike replied. "And you're right, of course. I just—" He stopped himself and turned to the fridge. "Do you want something?"

"No, I'm okay." The tightening was starting again, and she closed her eyes, willing her body to relax. She continued to rub her belly in slow circles as if calming the baby could somehow calm these pains, too. Was this due to stress?

"Why don't I throw together some lunch," Mike said, and Malory heard the sounds of him rummaging in the fridge. "I'm in the mood for omelets. What about you? Do you like breakfast for lunch?"

Malory's breathing was strenuous as the cramping began to pass once more, and when she opened her eyes, she found Mike looking at her, worry etched in his features.

"You're not okay," he pronounced and came back to her side, hunkering down next to her. "What's going on?"

"I don't know," she admitted. "But those twinges are getting worse." Another pain was coming on the heels of the last one, and while she had no idea what was going on, she knew that this wasn't a good sign.

"You need a doctor, Malory," he said, his voice low. "Are you in labor?"

"I don't know—" She clenched her teeth. "Maybe. Oh—" She pressed her lips together again, and Mike took her hands in his. She squeezed his fingers until the pain started to subside. When it passed, she opened her eyes to find Mike still looking into her face.

"Okay, first of all, ouch," he said. "You've got quite

the grip there. And secondly, you're going to a doctor. I'm just going to make a call first."

"What about Katy?"

Mike didn't answer and dialed his cell phone instead. After a few seconds, he said, "Hey, Tuck. I need a favor right now. I've got to get Malory to a doctor, and someone needs to take care of Katy for us—" He listened for a moment. "Yeah, labor, I think."

Labor? Was this it? Was she about to deliver her baby at five months? Had Mike seen this before? Would he know labor if it happened in the middle of his kitchen?

"You know the situation." Mike dropped his tone. "She needs protection, not just babysitting—" Another pause. "Actually, that would be perfect. Thanks, man. I owe you one."

Hanging up the phone, Mike glanced at his watch. "Tuck will be here in five minutes. He's putting the siren on and running stop signs."

"What's he going to do?" she asked weakly. "What about—?" She glanced at Katy, not wanting to even mention her criminal father.

"He's going to bring her to the station. She'll be in the middle of a whole bunch of deputies who will spoil her rotten."

Malory nodded. Katy stood by the table, her doll clutched around the neck as she stared at Malory with wide, frightened eyes.

"Nanny Mal?" Her little voice quavered.

"I'm okay, sweetie," Malory tried to reassure her. "But I have to see a doctor, okay? You're going to see

Mr. Tuck. You remember him. He was here yesterday, and he stayed with us."

The pain started again, and Malory closed her eyes and leaned forward. Everything else dissolved around her in the wake of the tightening pain. A small hand wormed over her leg, and Katy's trembling voice said, "Nanny Mal? Do you have an owie?"

Malory let out a long breath and she opened her eyes.

"Yes, I have an owie," she said as calmly as possible, then turned panic-stricken eyes toward the big man beside her. "Mike, get me to a hospital!"

Chapter Fifteen

Malory lay in the hospital bed, her eyes half-closed. Bright afternoon sunlight came in slices through the blinds. The room had two beds in it, but the other was empty, leaving Malory in relative privacy. Her bed was cranked up to keep her in a sitting position, a cord with a button at the end dangling by her head. Not that she'd need it. Mike had been by her side all afternoon, except for the times when the hospital staff pulled the curtain shut around her bed for privacy. But he never did leave—not completely. He'd be back again with a cup of tea or a snack for her to nibble on.

A crisp sheet and a thin hospital blanket covered her legs, an awkward hospital gown keeping her modest. Her hand ached where an IV pumped fluids into her body—the spot where the tube went in felt oddly cold. They'd tried to put the IV into her arm but couldn't get a vein, so while this spot wasn't comfortable, Malory knew better than to complain if she didn't want another nursing intern having a go at her arm again.

It had been a long afternoon consisting of a steady flow of strong medications and all the poking and prodding that came with hospital care. She was exhausted, but at least the contractions had stopped.

Mike sat by her bedside—right where he'd been the entire time. He wasn't looking at her—his gaze was focused somewhere in the middle of the floor, his thoughts clearly a mile away. Small lines creased the corners of his eyes, and she could make out a few grays in his short-cropped hair. His shirt strained at his biceps where he leaned forward, resting his elbows on his knees in that now-familiar position.

"What a day," Malory murmured.

"You can say that again." He offered her a smile. "How are you feeling?"

"Like I've been hit by a truck. How do I look?"

"Beautiful." His tone was quiet, and she didn't really believe him. Her hair was a mess, and she felt puffy and pale.

"You and your flattery." She laughed softly.

Mike reached out and took her hand, smoothing his thumb over her fingers, avoiding the tape that held her IV in place.

"I was scared there for a bit," he admitted.

"You didn't seem like it," she replied.

"That's the training. I'm supposed to look in control no matter what." His expression was rueful. "So I fake it well, do I?"

"Like a pro." She smiled at his joke, then took a slow breath. "I was afraid I'd give birth today."

"Me, too." His callused fingers moved carefully over hers, tracing her knuckles and down to her fingernails in slow, soothing movements.

"I wonder how Katy is," she said.

"She's fine." Mike released her hand and pulled out his cell phone. He held it up for her to see the picture Tuck had sent. It showed Katy sitting on his desk, a bag of chips in her hands and a grin on her face.

"Yes, that's some photo proof," she replied with a soft laugh. "Looks like she's enjoying herself."

"Told you they'd spoil her rotten."

A doctor came into the room, her eyes fixed on the clipboard in front of her. She paused in the doorway, flipping through the pages on the board. She was an older woman with chin-length white hair. She looked at Malory over her half-framed glasses, then gave Mike a friendly nod.

"Let's see…" Dr. Levato tapped the pages and gave her a maternal smile. "Nothing new on your chart. It's pretty simple, really. It seems that your baby is impatient."

"That's what I'm afraid of," Malory said weakly.

"Well, the baby is going to stay where he belongs for the time being—" She stopped. "Or she."

"I know it's a boy," Malory said.

"Thought I might have ruined the surprise," the doctor replied with a sheepish smile. "Well, as I was saying, he's going to stay put. We managed to stop labor, and his heartbeat is strong. How many weeks along are you?"

"Twenty," she replied.

The doctor nodded. "He needs more time on the inside, but I think you know that."

Her baby was right where he belonged, and she intended to keep him there as long as she possibly could, but the risk of his early delivery still left her feeling anxious.

"So he looks healthy?" she asked.

"Very," the doctor replied. "What you need is bed rest."

"Bed rest?" She opened her eyes in alarm. "I can't do bed rest—"

"You'll have to," Dr. Levato interrupted. "That doesn't mean you have to be literally in your bedroom for the next few months, but it does mean that you need to be sitting or lying down for the majority of your day. You can get up for a shower once a day, but other than that, I want you resting."

"What about cooking, child care—?"

"Someone else will have to do it. There is no saying we can stop labor the next time this happens, so it's your job to rest. That's your doctor's orders."

She sighed and nodded. This was the end of her job—that much was clear. She couldn't perform her duties as nanny while she was relaxing on a couch. Sadness welled up inside her. What would happen with Katy? What about Mike? Was this the end of every-thing for her here in Hope, Montana? She'd known all along that this was a temporary situation, but she'd expected a little more warning before it ended. She wasn't as ready for this as she'd thought she'd be.

She cast a helpless look in Mike's direction, but his expression was unreadable, hidden behind that mask of professional reserve.

"Are you working right now?" the doctor asked

cheerfully, scribbling on a page in a flourish of hand-writing.

"I'm a nanny," Malory replied. "So, yes."

"Ah." The doctor looked at Mike speculatively, one eyebrow arched. "Well, I'll provide all the documents and signatures that your workplace will require to get the time off work. I'll make sure you get everything before you leave the hospital."

"Thank you," she murmured.

"And, Mike—" the doctor turned toward the big cop "—can I talk to you?"

"You bet." Mike stood up, and on his way past, he gave her foot a gentle squeeze. They stepped outside the room, Mike pulling the door gently shut behind him, leaving Malory in quiet.

The baby moved inside her, and she put a hand on her belly, thankful that her boy was healthy and safe. That was the top priority here, but her heart still deflated with sadness. They still needed her. Katy needed stability, and Malory wanted to be able to provide it for her for as long as possible. Mike could use some support, too, whether he knew it or not, and she didn't want to just get on the next bus out of their lives, never to see them again.

But that was the job—she'd always been a temporary solution.

Yet they'd become more to her than just a job in this short period of time. Perhaps it was the drama of the break-ins, but they'd pulled together in a different way than she normally experienced as a nanny. They were leaning on each other, relying on each other. They felt more like a family.

That wasn't the way things were supposed to go, and she'd been warned about maintaining appropriate boundaries in her training with the agency.

This is why, she thought miserably. It hurt too much when it all came to an end.

MIKE STOOD WITH the doctor in the hallway. Dr. Levato's expression was grim.

"I don't like to scare the mother in these situations, but it's imperative that she stay off her feet. Whatever her job, she can't go back, even for a couple of days."

"Understood." Mike nodded. This certainly complicated things with Katy, but he'd figure something out.

"She's healthy, and so is the baby, but her body seems to want to deliver early, so I'm leaving this in your hands."

Mike frowned. "I'm not sure that Malory will like that much," he admitted.

"Then make it pleasant for her," the doctor replied. "You'll find a way, I'm sure. If she gets up to do so much as fetch the remote, I'm holding you personally responsible."

"That's a tall order." Mike chuckled.

"I suppose I should also offer my congratulations," the older woman said with a smile. "I hadn't realized you were involved with someone, but—"

"No, no." Mike shook his head. "I'm not the father. This isn't my child."

"Oh." She seemed taken aback. "That is certainly

more complicated, but I'm sure you'll be able to sort it out. You're a good man."

Mike frowned. "No, she's my nanny. That's all. We aren't anything more."

"I apologize." Dr. Levato's face turned pink. "I just assumed by the way you two... You were by her side for hours, and—" She cleared her throat. "But she is living at your home?"

"Yes, it's a live-in position," Mike said. "And I'll do what I can to make sure she stays off her feet, but I doubt she'll stay long. She'll probably want to go home so she can have her baby closer to her family."

The doctor eyed Mike speculatively and put a hand on his arm. "And you'd be all right with that?"

Mike sighed. "It isn't my choice to make."

"I'm just saying, the way you stayed with her, calmed her, brought her food—" She paused, meeting Mike's gaze. "I just thought I sensed something more there."

"She doesn't have anyone else in Hope," Mike replied. "I'm just doing what I can."

The doctor nodded. "Fair enough. But I stand by what I said—not so much as fetching the remote. Understood?"

"Understood." Mike laughed. "Are you going to release her today?"

The doctor scribbled on the bottom of her chart and passed the clipboard over. "I've signed off on it. The rest is up to you."

"Thanks, Doctor."

"Take care, Mike." She squeezed his shoulder.

"And good to see you—without needing stitches or anything."

Mike laughed at her dark humor. "Absolutely."

The doctor shook Mike's hand and then headed into the next room, picking up the next chart on her way in, leaving Mike alone in the hallway.

Mike was used to being responsible for the people of Hope, and Malory was no different. It didn't matter if he was attracted to her or if he even had feelings for her. What mattered was that she was alone and she needed someone to support her—even if she wished she didn't.

A sheriff served and protected. And that was what he was doing.

Wasn't it?

Chapter Sixteen

Mike sat at the kitchen table with Katy. She clutched a green crayon in her fist, a coloring book in front of her. The picture was of a rainbow and a cow, all of which had been scribbled over in green.

Mike had a coloring book in front of him, too, and he looked down at his handiwork. It was surprisingly therapeutic to color a picture, and he could now see why kids liked it so much.

"Do you want my purple crayon?" Mike offered.

"No. I like green," came the reply.

He smiled and shook his head. She certainly had her own ideas, and he liked that about her. She was all personality and she wouldn't be easily pushed around.

"Uncle Mike, I'm hungry."

"Do you think Nanny Mal is hungry, too?" Mike asked.

"I dunno."

"Go ask her."

Katy scampered out of the kitchen and into the living room, where Malory lay on the couch.

"Are you hungry, Nanny Mal?" he heard her ask. "Nanny Mal?"

Mike craned his neck to see around the corner. Malory was fast asleep, her arm resting on a magazine. She'd been thoroughly annoyed to be banished to the couch only an hour before, but now it looked as if the prescription had had its desired effect, and she was relaxing even more than she'd intended. Out cold, mouth slack and was that a tiny bit of drool? He grinned. She was adorable when she slept—not that he'd dare tell her that.

"Katy, let's let Nanny Mal sleep," Mike said. "Come over here and I'll make you something. What do you want?"

Katy poked at Malory a couple more times, then gave up and returned to the kitchen.

"Goldfish crackers," she announced.

"Hmm." He opened the cupboard. "That's more of a snack. I was thinking of feeding you a whole meal."

"Lots of Goldfish crackers!"

Mike chuckled. "Hold on.... How about macaroni and cheese?"

He pulled out a box and held it down for her. Katy nodded enthusiastically, and Mike grabbed a pot and filled it with water.

"Did you have fun today?" he asked her.

"Yup." She stood on tiptoe, trying to see what he was doing, small fingertips squeezed against the countertop.

"What did you do with Mr. Tuck?" he asked.

"I licked his phone," she said with an impish grin, and Mike burst out laughing.

"Did he like that?"

"No."

He doubted anyone would like that, but if anyone could take it in stride, it would be Tuck. He had the feeling that Katy wasn't the first kid to lick his phone.

"Did you get to play with the siren in the police car?" he asked.

She looked up blankly.

"The big light that went—" And he whooped for her benefit, imitating the sound of a squad-car siren.

"Uh-huh!" She nodded excitedly. "And I used a stapler!"

"You did?"

The phone rang, and Mike pulled down some Goldfish crackers and shook a few out onto a plate, grabbing the handset as he worked.

"Hello?" He passed the plate to Katy. "Here, have a few crackers while you wait," he said, and she joyfully grabbed the plate, sending half of them bouncing across the tile floor.

"Hi, sorry about that. Mike here."

"Hello, this is Elizabeth Nelson from the adoption agency."

Just like that, the joy in the moment came crashing down, and Mike scrubbed a hand through his short hair. Katy crouched on the floor, picking up crackers and depositing them back onto her plate, and he didn't have the heart to stop her.

"Hi, how are you?" he said.

"Just great. I got a call from the Petersens, and they were more than impressed with Katy when they met her."

"That's great," Mike said, trying to sound more enthusiastic than he felt.

"In fact, they want to take her. They felt a connection with her at your home the other day, and they've made their decision."

Mike cleared his throat. "As quickly as that?"

"Yes, apparently so. Why, are you concerned about anything?" She sounded cautious. "I do appreciate your insights both as a sheriff and as Katy's guardian."

"I'm sure you've screened them," he said.

"Very thoroughly, both through the police and a private detective. They are exactly as they appear to be—a successful couple with a lot of love to give."

Mike sighed. What were his reservations about the couple—that their pants matched? That they were mildly annoying in just how perfect they were? That they could provide everything she could possibly need or want, while he felt as though the little he had to offer could never hold up? His real problem was that he didn't want to let go of her, and he knew it.

"No, they're good people and they seem to have everything she needs," he admitted.

"Are you reconsidering giving Katy up?" the woman pressed. "If you need to take more time, that's okay, you know. It's better to take things more slowly than to make a decision you regret."

Taking his time wouldn't change anything. Sinclair Moody was still out there, and he'd still come for Katy.

Mike was willing to bet on that. Katy needed a home as far from her biological father's grasp as possible, and this well-educated couple was the ideal solution.

"No." Mike dumped the boxed noodles into the boiling water. "This is hard for me—I won't try to hide it—but the circumstances aren't going to change. This is what is best for Katy."

"I'll tell you what," the woman said, sympathy in her tone. "You have until they drive away with her to change your mind. I'll let them know that you are agreeing but still have a few reservations, just so they'll know what to expect."

"That sounds fair," Mike agreed.

Was he really undecided? Having the finality of the decision put off helped to ease some of his discomfort.

"Thanks," he said. "When should I expect them?"

"They'd like to come tomorrow to start the transition," Ms. Nelson replied. "If that is okay with you."

"That would be fine," he agreed. "Thanks. We'll see you then."

Hanging up the phone, Mike stood in front of the stove, staring down into the bubbling water. This had all happened so quickly—first Katy's arrival, and now her exit. He wished there were a way to keep her for longer, but he knew that reality wouldn't allow for it. This was part of the Cruise curse, the constant contact with the unsavory parts of society, and Katy's connection was even more sordid than his own.

She deserved a life away from this ugliness. She deserved a life safe from Sinclair Moody. And she deserved two loving parents to dote on her. Why was he wanting to hold her back?

For me, he realized. For once in his life, he'd bonded with another Cruise who wasn't already swallowed up by addiction and crime. And that felt more comforting than he cared to admit.

"Uncle Mike?" Katy held up her plate. "More?"

"Hold on, kiddo," he said, trying to sound cheerier than he felt. "These noodles are done, and I just have to mix in the cheese."

"Cheeeeese…" she intoned, and he laughed softly. He turned off the heat and squatted down next to her.

"Katy?" he said quietly.

She looked at him, big blue eyes fixed on his face.

"Will you do your very best to remember me?" he asked. "Will you always remember that your Uncle Mike loves you?"

She squished up her face, not understanding what he was getting at. It was better that way anyhow. She didn't need the weight of the world on her small shoulders when his were plenty broad enough to hoist it for her.

"Never mind, kiddo," he said, tousling her hair and standing up. "You're hungry, aren't you?"

Mike drained the noodles and added in a splash of milk and the packet of dry cheese. As he stirred, his sadness welled up, threatening to break past his careful reserve. His hands moved as if on their own, going through the motions of making macaroni and cheese.

"Uncle Mike?"

Mike looked down, giving her what he hoped was a reassuring smile. "Yes?"

"Can I call you Daddy now?" Katy asked quietly, and he as he looked down at her, he wished with all his heart that his answer could be different.

"That isn't a good idea, kiddo," he replied, his throat tight. "You'll have a daddy real soon, and you should save that name for him."

The sparkle in her eyes evaporating, she stared at him for a long moment, her expression empty, and then she started to cry. She turned her face away from him, not letting him see. She felt his rejection.

Nice, he thought miserably. *And now you get to break her heart, too.*

LATER THAT EVENING, with Katy tucked in, watching a children's TV program on Mike's tablet, Mike came down the stairs to check on Malory.

"What's going on?" Malory asked from her position on the couch, rubbing her hands over her eyes. "What did I miss?"

Mike sank down next to her, and she pulled her legs up to give him space.

"I got a call from the adoption agency," he said, "and the Petersens are more than interested—they want to take Katy."

Malory swallowed and looked away for a moment. "So soon?" she asked.

"Yeah, that's what I asked, too." He smiled sadly. "The thing is, they're good people. They've been vetted and screened. They have everything to offer her."

"And I'm sure you've looked into them, too," she added.

He chuckled. "They're as squeaky-clean as you are."

Malory nodded slowly. "And they're unrelated to the Cruises in any way."

"A point in their favor."

"So—" She faltered. "What did you say?"

Mike didn't answer at first. Then he heaved a sigh and turned his dark eyes to meet hers.

"I said okay."

He'd agreed. Of course, there was no reason why he shouldn't. This had been the plan all along, but the finality of the decision weighed her down.

"So what do you think?" he asked, his gaze trained on her as if she held some sort of key to release him from his misery.

"I don't know what to say," she replied, tears filling her eyes. "I'm sad."

"Me, too."

"And you're sure about this?" Malory asked.

"Not really. I'm conflicted, but I want to put Katy first. This isn't about me. She's not my daughter, but I still have to be the one to decide what's right for her. Hardly seems fair, does it?"

"Have you told her yet?" Malory asked.

"Not yet. I wanted your help with that. I don't know how to tell her…what to tell her. And it's all so fast."

"I suppose the timing is rather good, too," Malory admitted. "The doctor was clear that I can't keep working, so I'll be leaving soon, too."

"I wasn't really wanting to face that just yet." He

rubbed his hand over his short hair. "You can stay, you know."

"You know I can't."

"Well—" He looked like he was considering his next words carefully. "I mean, for as long as you need to. Don't feel rushed. Take it easy. Rest up. I'm not speeding you out of here."

Malory nodded. "Thanks. I appreciate that."

She wasn't in an incredible rush to move in with her mother and her fiancé, either, but she didn't have many options right now, and staying longer with Mike was only putting off the inevitable. And playing house, in a way. It was better to face reality than to avoid it with a handsome sheriff. That was what he was doing with his own situation, wasn't it? He was facing reality, even if it hurt.

"When are they coming for Katy?" she asked.

"Tomorrow morning."

"That's not a lot of time to get her adjusted to the idea."

"No, but she hasn't been here long, either. I'm sure the adoption agency will have a few suggestions on how to make the transition easier for her." He shook his head. "She'd have all the advantages, but do you really think that they'd be the right fit for her?"

"You're thinking of fuchsia tracksuits again, aren't you?" Malory attempted to lighten the mood.

"Yes." He smiled wryly. "Is this the right decision? What if they don't understand her? What if she grows up with all the newest toys and the best schools but never really connects with them?"

"That's what family therapy is for," she suggested. "To help them bond."

"Does she even like them?" he asked, but he didn't seem to expect an answer. They could hear Katy's laughter upstairs. "The other option is to stay with me. And we all know how safe she is here."

"Safer than you think," Malory countered. "I don't think a whole lot could get through you."

"A bullet would." The grim determination in his voice sent a shiver down her spine. "I can't be vigilant every second. I have to sleep, too. If this guy wanted to get at her, all he'd have to do was wait long enough... wait until I let my guard down. No, she has to be away from him completely."

"So what are your options?" she asked.

"Well, I can let her go to the Petersens, or I can wait a little longer and see if there is another family that is less matchy-matchy." He shot her a droll smile. "I know, it's stupid. I know what I have to do. I just don't have to like it."

"Mike?" He turned back toward her and she put a hand on his muscled arm. "You're a good guy, you know."

He didn't answer, and he looked away again. Silence filled the room, broken only by the sound of the TV show and Katy's giggles from upstairs.

"How can I help?" she asked at last.

"You can help me break the news," he replied.

Malory nodded.

"I'll bring her down." Mike rose to his feet.

He gave her hand a squeeze, then let it drop and

headed toward the stairs. As he went up, Malory began to cry.

This was it. She shouldn't have gotten this attached, but she had, and now she had to summon up the strength to see it through to the end. Katy needed to see that everything would be okay, and she'd look to Malory for confirmation of that.

There was no time for tears when children needed your strength.

Chapter Seventeen

That night, after Malory and Katy were already asleep, Mike sat in the living room alone. He just couldn't bring himself to lie down yet—his protective instinct kicking into high gear for one last night. Sometimes steeling himself for attack was easier than facing the depths of his own sadness.

Katy had understood better than he'd thought. She'd have a new family—a new mommy and a new daddy—and they would take very good care of her. She liked the Petersens. When informed that she would be their little girl, she'd looked at the doll in a whole new way. Her tiny brows had knit together, and she'd stared down at the plastic face as if it had betrayed her somehow. She seemed to sense that she'd been bought off.

This wasn't the way it was supposed to be, although what exactly he'd expected, he couldn't say.

Outside, a car's motor rumbled up the drive, and Mike went to the window and nudged aside the curtain to look out. It was a black Crown Victoria, outlined in the moonlight. Two large men got out first. Then one opened the door to the backseat and Nate climbed out, pausing in the silvery darkness. He looked quickly around himself, then came toward the front door.

What was his father doing here at this hour of night with two FBI agents? The two bruisers couldn't be anything else. He hadn't set Nate free yet, and these guys had that federally trained look about them and they moved in formation, staying behind Nate to keep him protected. Their suit jackets wore as if there was bulletproofing underneath them.

As if Mrs. McNaughton from across the street would have a sniper in her front room. The thought brought a wry smile to his lips, but lately he wouldn't put anything out of the realm of possible—at least where Sinclair Moody was concerned.

Mike opened the front door before his father had a chance to ring the bell, and they regarded each other in silence for several seconds before Nate said, "Could I come in?"

"What's this about, Dad?" Mike asked.

"I have some explaining to do," Nate said.

Mike stepped back and Nate came inside, followed by the two agents. They flashed their badges—FBI, as he'd suspected—and then stood by the door, arms crossed over massive chests. Mike was used to being considered a rather big man, but next to these guys, he was downright average.

"Come in," Mike sighed, jutting his chin in the direction of the couch. "So what brings you over here at this time of night?"

"They said it was better this way—" Nate nodded

toward the FBI agents. "I'm going to disappear for a while, son."

"How long?" Mike asked.

Nate swallowed, and Mike thought he could detect tears in his father's eyes, but he couldn't be sure in the low light.

"For good, kid," he said gruffly.

Mike frowned. "What's happening, exactly?"

"I'm testifying against Sinclair Moody in court."

"You are?" Mike stared at his father in shock. "That's a dangerous thing to do, Dad. Are you sure about this?"

"I know stuff, and Mr. Moody knows that." Nate shrugged. "I'm not safe either way."

Mike could see that was true, but he still didn't like the idea of his father being used for testimony that would leave him a target for a heartless criminal.

"I'll get a new life, a new start. Somewhere far from here."

"What about Gina? Is she even real?"

"Yeah, she's real. She's…she's a good woman. Better than I deserve."

"Will she go with you?" Mike asked.

The older man shook his head. "She'll think I just left one day. It'll hurt. Might not surprise her too much. She'll think I couldn't clean up my act after all, and she'd be right."

"So you're giving up your girlfriend, your life, everything. And that means—" Mike heard the gruffness enter his tone "—that means you'll never see me again, either."

Nate nodded sullenly. "I wasn't much of a dad anyway."

"But you're still my dad."

"Look, kid." Nate leaned forward. "I don't like this, either. But I've got to do what's right once in my life. There's no going back. They've already got Moody in custody, and everything is going forward. After the trial, I disappear." He snapped his fingers. "Puff of smoke."

Mike glanced toward the two FBI agents. "Is that true? Is Moody in custody?"

"It's true," came the curt reply.

Conflicting emotions warred within him. His father might have been a hot mess when he was growing up, but at least he had a father. Now his dad would vanish—really vanish—and he'd never be able to contact him again. He'd always known that at his father's funeral he would grieve deeply, regardless of how damaged his father had been, and it seemed as if that moment of grief was now.

"I don't know how to say goodbye." Mike cleared his throat.

Nate nodded, his gaze on the floor. "I know you don't like me much, kiddo, but I love you."

Mike said nothing. He didn't know how to answer his father. He knew how to get angry. He knew how to avoid a situation, but he didn't know how to say goodbye on a dime. His father had been a negligent parent, an addict and a poor role model, but at least Mike had known his dad. That was something.

"Mike, I always meant to shape up one day." Nate's

voice was surprisingly steady. "I was going to make it up to you. I was."

"It's okay." Mike scrubbed a hand through his hair.

"Not really," Nate disagreed. "So this is my chance to do things right by you. I was the idiot who got involved with Sinclair Moody, and that put you in danger. Now, if it weren't for you, I wouldn't be testifying, I can promise you that. But this isn't about what I want, or what's easy for me. This is about my son, for once. I don't know how you turned out so good, kid, but you did, in spite of me. This time I want to protect you."

Mike was big and broad, muscular and solid, while his father was almost frail in comparison. His gray hair stood up in uncombed tufts, and his chin was covered in week-old silver stubble. He wrung his grease-stained hands in the silence.

"I don't think that's really wise, Dad," Mike muttered.

"Wise or not, you're still my son."

"I'm in a better position to protect you right now," Mike replied.

"That's not the way it's supposed to be, Mike." Nate's eyes flashed fire. "Let me do it right for once."

Was his father serious? Would he really testify and allow himself to be tucked away behind God's back somewhere, giving up everything he knew to put one scumbag behind bars? Mike tried to swallow the lump that rose in his throat. "How do I know if you're okay?"

"How did you know before?" Nate retorted.

"So this is it?" Mike asked. "Goodbye forever?"

Nate nodded, tears sparkling in his eyes. "But before I go, I have to tell you that I'm sorry. I should have straightened up before—when it would have made a difference for you and me."

"Better late than never, I guess."

"Do you—?" Nate shifted uncomfortably. "Do you forgive me?"

"Yeah."

Nate leaned forward and put an arm around Mike's neck, pulling him into an awkward hug. Mike stayed there for a long moment, his face against his father's thin neck, smelling that combination of grease and cigarette smoke that he'd always associated with the man. Then his father released him and stood quickly to his feet.

"Okay, well," Nate said gruffly. "This one is for you, okay? For you."

Mike rose to his feet as his father went toward the door. "Dad?"

Nate turned, tears on his weathered cheeks. "Yeah?"

"I love you, too."

Nate nodded. "I know." He raised his hand in an impotent little wave, then followed the first agent out the door, sandwiched by the second. As quickly as they'd arrived, they were leaving. Mike stood in the doorway, the cool summer air caressing his face as the agent slammed shut the back door to the car and then got into the driver's seat. Mike couldn't see into the backseat where his father sat—the windows were all tinted black.

Was his father looking at him?

He waved, then let his hand drop.

There had been a time, a long time ago, when Mike had fantasized about his father going away and staying away—his father had been absent for the past ten years, so it didn't really change anything except the possibility of his reappearance. His dad would never be back. What he wouldn't give for a few more weeks with his father around.

"Bye, Dad—" The tears rose up in his throat and cut off his words. The car backed out of the drive and disappeared in a swirl of dust down the road. For the first time in Nate's life, he'd done something for his son without any thoughts for himself.

At least Nate was going out as a father.

Mike heard a rustle behind him and he turned to see Malory at the bottom of the stairs. Tears glistened in her eyes. She crossed the room and wrapped her arms around him, leaning her cheek against his chest. She didn't speak, didn't ask anything of him, just held him in a warm, gentle embrace. She'd seen it all, and he was relieved not to have to explain this one. He slid his arms around her, and he realized as he stroked her silky hair that despite her difficult pregnancy and delicate frame, she was the strongest one in the room right now. He needed her strength just as much as she needed his.

A few minutes later, Mike mounted the stairs. The next day, the Petersens would come to see their new daughter, and he'd also do the right thing and put a little girl's needs ahead of his own. With Sinclair Moody behind bars, she'd be safe from her biological father, but Mike could do one better and free her from the Cruises completely.

She'd have a life of matching tracksuits and devoted parents, and God willing, she'd never remember the messy life of crime and ugliness that she came from.

EARLY THE NEXT MORNING, Malory sat on the window seat in her white nightgown, the pink morning light flooding over her. She smoothed one hand over her belly, humming softly to her baby.

The night had been a restless one. After she'd witnessed Mike's goodbye with his father, she'd lain awake, listening to the groan of the house shifting, the sound of the wind in the leaves.

When dawn finally came, she'd gotten up, but remembering the doctor's orders, she sat on the window seat and watched the world as it was bathed in pink light, then soft gold. She turned at a creak on the floorboards in the hallway to see Mike standing there, fully dressed.

"Did you go to bed at all?" Malory asked.

He shook his head. "I meant to, but it didn't happen."

"It's a new day," she said quietly. "My mother used to say that everything looked better in morning light."

"Does it?" he asked.

"Come see." She gestured for him to join her, and he came slowly into the room, then carefully lowered himself onto the little seat beside her. He looked out the window at the peaceful scene.

"I've been thinking a lot," Mike said quietly.

"What about?"

The sunlight was growing stronger, and with the

morning rays came the joyful twittering of birds outside.

"About us," he said.

Malory smiled wistfully. So had she, truth be told, but her thoughts had been wishes and fantasies—something that was much clearer to her now that she was in daylight.

"Mike, we shouldn't go there—"

"I think we should." He caught her gaze and held it. "Look, all of this is ending so quickly, and I'm not ready for that."

"Whoever is?" she asked with a slight shrug. "I'll miss you."

"Me, too. But what if we didn't have to end it?"

With the jumble of events, she hadn't really thought about what Nate's gesture would mean for her. The danger was past—Moody in FBI custody.

Malory froze, a wave of longing coursing over her. Was the drama really all over? She wished that she could say yes, that she could just lose herself in this little town called Hope, that she could wake up to mornings like this one every single day and exist in this dream world. But she couldn't.

"Mike, I can't do that." She shook her head. "This isn't my life. It's yours."

"We could see where things went. Maybe you'd want to make it your life, too."

An image flashed in Malory's mind of her mother, standing before a full-length mirror as she got ready for a date. Malory, a young child at the time, watched her mother putting in her earrings, and her mother was saying, "I have a good feeling about this one, sweetie pie..."

Her mother always had a good feeling about the men she dated. She always thought that each one of them had the potential to be Mr. Right. She'd never seen it coming—even after the fifth or sixth time her Mr. Right walked out the door.

Sitting here in the morning light, she could understand her mother's optimism, because she shared it—but there was a difference... Malory was wiser than her mother had been.

"No." She swallowed back the lump rising in her throat. "I'm sorry, Mike. I'm going home."

He was silent for a moment, and he leaned forward, elbows resting on his knees.

"When are you leaving?" he asked.

"Today."

"Seriously?" He straightened. "So soon? Why not stay a few more days?"

"It's better this way," she replied.

"Why?" He frowned. "Look, Malory, you were only in the hospital a few days ago. Don't you think you owe it to yourself to rest a bit?"

"No." She sighed, wrapping her arms around herself. "I don't. The longer I stay here—" She bit back the words.

"What?" he prompted. "The longer you stay here, what?"

"The more attached I get to—to this life—to—" She didn't know how to pull it all together into words.

"Malory, it's okay to get attached. I can take care of you."

"I'm not your duty, Mike," she replied, her tone sharper than she intended. But she meant it.

"Who said you were?"

"The whole town is your duty." She jutted her chin in the direction of the window. "Everyone here. You take care of this town like a mother hen. I'm not one your chicks."

He laughed softly. "Do I really mollycoddle you that much?" His tone suggested that he wasn't buying it.

"I don't need special treatment," she retorted, attempting to control her rising voice. "You don't get it, do you? I don't want this. I want to go home."

Mike froze before his expression turned to granite once more. Malory hated the professional reserve that he hid behind, making her feel like the emotional one, when she knew that he was feeling just as much as she was.

"I don't get you," he said at last. "A man treats you properly, and you fight it tooth and nail. What have I done that's so wrong? I was considerate. I tried to make you comfortable."

"You gave me special treatment because I'm pregnant!"

"And good thing, too!" he fired back. "You were in the hospital, remember?"

"Let's be perfectly clear," she replied, unable to control the quiver in her voice. "I don't need a man to take care of me. The break-ins and all that—I needed a sheriff to keep me safe, but my personal life is another matter. In my personal life, I'm taking care of myself."

"Are you sure about this?"

"Yes!" She stood up, then remembered again the doctor's orders and sat back down grumpily. "Yes." She shook her head. "It might be hard right now. It might be hard for a really long time, but I don't need anyone else to swoop in and rescue me. I'm fine. I can do this."

"Okay." He stood up, the mask disintegrating. Pain flickered deep in his dark gaze. "Just tell me straight— do you feel what I do? Because I'm falling for you, Malory."

She looked away, tears in her eyes, then heaved a sigh. "It doesn't matter what I feel, Mike. I know what I have to do."

"And why wouldn't your feelings matter?" he demanded, shaking his head. "If you feel what I do—"

"Because I saw my mother do this again and again and again, and I swore to myself I would never become her!"

She remembered her mother, sitting on the side of her bed, sniffling into a crumpled tissue as her mascara ran down her cheeks in inky trails. Malory would stand there feeling helpless. She'd known what the problem was from a young age—her mother thought she needed these random boyfriends. She'd thought that they would solve all her problems. But Malory and her mom hadn't needed these men at all—they'd needed each other. She'd needed her mother, her strong, happy, confident mother, not the broken, dejected soul who sat on the edge of her bed weeping out her misery into a sodden tissue.

Mike shook his head in frustration.

"Okay," he said. "If you change your mind—"

"I won't," she said quickly, swallowing her doubt.

He nodded, then turned and walked out of the room, leaving her alone with the morning sunlight, the birds and that seat beside the window.

Never before had she realized just how hard it would be to become someone different. She leaned her forehead against the cool glass, and the tears that had been trapped for what felt like days finally spilled down her cheeks.

But under all that sadness and fear, under the tears that kept coming, she finally admitted what she'd been shoving down all this time—she was in love with that burly sheriff with the heart of gold. It was good to acknowledge why this hurt so badly. But it didn't change anything.

Chapter Eighteen

"Good morning." Mike forced a smile and stepped back as the Petersens and the adoption agent came inside. The couple looked around nervously while Ms. Nelson gave a professional smile and nod. They all stood next to Malory's bags, which sat ready by the door.

Just the sight of those bags made his heart ache. It was all ending today—all of it. He'd go right back to being the most eligible bachelor in the county, his home quiet and undisturbed. And he hated it.

"This is a big day," Belinda said, sucking in a deep breath. "Is she awake yet?"

"Yeah, she's just in there." He gestured them into the living room.

"We got her room ready last night," Belinda went on. "It's all pink—a ballerina theme. I think she'll love it."

Ned nodded, his gaze locked on Mike. "And how are you?" he asked. Could the doctor sense Mike's reluctance?

"I'm good, thanks." Mike hoped that his expression didn't betray the complicated emotions boiling inside him. His issues today weren't their problem. They were here to enlarge their family, and he was supposed to help them do it.

The couple moved over to the couch and sat down, their knees lined up like last time, their jeans the exact same shade of blue denim. They nodded to Malory, who sat in the easy chair, her legs tucked up. Katy sat on Malory's lap, her green dress crinkled up around her hips as she stared at the Petersens distrustfully.

"Hi, Katy," Belinda said softly.

Malory's smile was strained, and Mike didn't blame her. This certainly wasn't a happy day—not for them, at least.

"We're so thrilled to see you today, Katy." Belinda smiled. "Do you know why we're here?"

Katy nodded.

"Why?" Belinda asked softly.

"You're going to be my mommy and daddy."

"That's right," Ned chimed in gently. "And we're really happy that you're going to be our little girl."

Katy didn't answer, but she looked up at Malory, her eyes wide. Mike had to stifle the urge to step between them and bodily block their view of Katy. Ms. Nelson noticed Katy's reluctance, as well, and she leaned forward, taking control of the conversation.

"I'd like to make sure that Katy is comfortable before we discuss how we're going to do this," Ms. Nelson said. "We could start with a few overnight visits, if that makes things easier. Either Katy could come back here for a few days in between to help with the transition, or, Mike, you could go and visit her at her new

home. But we'll be able to talk about that a bit more
as we go on..."

The conversation continued—the Petersens talking about the preparations they had made, pulling out
a present for Katy. Katy wasn't lured over this time,
even when Malory encouraged her, whispering in her
ear that it would be all right. And as Mike watched the
scene unfold, he couldn't help but wonder if he wasn't
making a monumental mistake.

His father was willing to sacrifice in order to be a
good dad, just once, but what if Katy didn't need this
sacrifice? What if, instead of sacrificing his own longing to keep the little girl in his home, Mike just stepped
up to be the dad she needed?

"Katy, come see what I brought you," Belinda urged.
"It's a teddy bear. I used to play with a teddy bear just
like this one when I was a little girl like you."

Katy shook her head, tears in her eyes. "No. I don't
want it."

Belinda let the bear drop to her lap. This wasn't easy
on them, either, Mike could see.

Katy inched slowly down from Malory's lap, but
instead of moving toward the Petersens, she dashed
to Mike and latched on to his leg.

"Hey, kiddo," Mike said quietly and lifted her up
into his arms. She was still as light as a feather, her thin
arms wrapped around his neck tightly. She pressed her
cheek against his, and she trembled ever so slightly.

"Uncle Mike," she whispered in a little voice. "Why
can't you be my daddy?"

Mike couldn't stop his tears, and he wrapped his

arms around her. What could he say? He should put her down, but he found that he couldn't. Either she wouldn't let go, or he wouldn't, but neither of them moved.

His father might be sacrificing everything for Mike, and while he'd been so certain that a life away from the Cruises was the best thing for Katy, another thought occurred to him. When he was growing up in the middle of all that chaos and addiction, while he dreamed of a day that his father would just leave and never come back, he might have been better off dreaming of a day when his father could kick the alcohol and be the father he desperately needed. Sometimes the answer wasn't to stand strong alone—sometimes the best solution was to stand strong together. Maybe Katy didn't have to stop being a Cruise to be safe from the family curse.

"I—" He cleared his throat. "I think I've made a mistake."

The room descended into silence, and all eyes turned to Mike. The Petersens braced, as if waiting for terrible news, but the adoption agent appeared relatively unfazed. It was Malory's gentle gaze that drew him, and he met her eyes as the words came out.

"I thought I was doing Katy a favor by finding her a family away from my own, but I'm not sure that's the case anymore."

"It might be hard," Ned broke in. "I know it's hard, but think of Katy. Think of all we can offer her."

"I am thinking of Katy." Mike shook his head. "She's a Cruise, and that's not going to change, but we can certainly change this branch of the family tree. I'm going to keep her and I'm going to raise her myself."

Malory put her hands up to cover her mouth, but he could see her joyful tears.

"You'll be my daddy now?" Katy asked, hope in her voice.

"Yes, kiddo," Mike said gruffly. "I'll be your daddy now."

With a squeal, Katy hugged him close, her moist little face pressed into his neck as she wriggled in for the closest hug she could manage.

"Are you sure about this?" Ms. Nelson asked softly, putting a hand on his arm.

"Positive." He offered the Petersens an apologetic smile. "I'm sorry. I know this won't be easy on you."

"It's okay." Ned nodded curtly, and they rose from the couch. "Our hopes were up, but I understand."

Mike shook hands with the Petersens, holding Katy in his left arm, and the adoption agent led them toward the door. After some awkward goodbyes, Katy, Malory and Mike were left alone.

"Mike, this is amazing." Malory smiled, and she slipped her arms around his waist and put her face next to Katy's. "You'll be very happy together, you two."

"Will you be my mommy, Nanny Mal?" Katy asked hopefully.

Malory shook her head. "I'm sorry, sweetie, but I won't be."

"Why not?" Katy persisted.

"Because Nanny Mal is going to have a baby," Mike said gently. "And she has to go back to her own home.

So it'll be you and me, kiddo. We'll be okay, though, won't we?"

A car drove up outside the house, and Mike followed Malory's gaze out the window. His stomach sank. It was her cab—already.

"Look, Malory." He wished he had the words to express what he was feeling. "I know this isn't good timing, but—" he moved her hair away from her face "—I love you."

"Me, too," she whispered, and his heart thrilled at those words. So she loved him, too—he wasn't alone. If only it could end differently. She took a deep breath and stepped back.

"You sure you won't stay a little longer?" he asked hopefully.

She shook her head. "If I do, I'll never leave. I have to go, Mike."

She was forcing herself to walk away—he could see that much. Mike put Katy back down and picked up Malory's luggage.

"Let me bring your bags out," he said.

Malory followed him out the door. She gave Katy another hug, and after her bags were stowed in the trunk, she stood by the cab, trembling.

"Bye," she said softly. "I'm going to miss you, Mike."

He bent down and wrapped his arms around her. She was small in his embrace, even with her expanding belly, and he inhaled her soft scent. She leaned her face into his neck, and she grabbed handfuls of his shirt as she squeezed him back. He didn't want to let go of her, but she pulled away, and he reluctantly released her.

"I know you won't let me take care of you," he said gruffly, "but let someone, okay?"

She nodded quickly. He met her gaze one last time, and he wished he could lean in and kiss those lips again—but he didn't dare.

Even with Katy by his side, his heart was tied to Malory.

"To the airport, miss?" the driver asked through the open window.

"Yes, please," she said, but she found her voice not as stable as she would have liked. She was glad—deeply happy—that Mike was keeping Katy. She'd believed all along that those two belonged together, and walking away from them was harder than she'd ever imagined it would be.

This was for her baby, though. This was the stability that she never got as a child. She'd raise him herself, and he'd never know that rocking, terrified feeling of having his world tipped upside down every time his mother thought she might have found Mr. Right.

This is what I have to do, she reminded herself, but deep down, it hurt so much that she wondered if she wasn't making a mistake, too.

Mike reached for the door to open it for her, and she shook her head.

"I can do this," she reassured him, and he paused.

"Okay." He stepped back. "Take care, Mal."

"You, too." Her words caught in her throat. "Katy, you be a good girl for your dad, okay?"

She gathered the girl into her arms and hugged her close.

"Bye, Nanny Mal."

"Bye, sweetie."

Katy didn't want to let go, but after a moment, she pulled back and asked, "Will you miss me?"

"With all my heart," Malory whispered. She swallowed hard. "Now it's time to go back inside, okay?"

Mike took Katy's hand. With one last look, he turned and led the girl—his daughter—toward the porch. The cab driver cranked up his radio as a highway traffic report came on, and at that moment, another car careened into the drive, the sound of the tires drowned out by the voices on the radio.

The car stopped, and the door opened almost simultaneously. The glint of a gun reflected in the sunlight, and Malory's heart nearly stopped. The only thing she could think of was Mike and Katy, their backs turned as they climbed the steps to the front porch. For all of her fear of needing a man, Mike and Katy now needed *her*, and there was no way she was letting anything happen to them while she had breath in her body.

"Mike!" she shouted. "Mike!"

The man froze, then turned toward her, the gun now pointed directly at her. She didn't have time to say another word, and her heart leaped to her throat as she realized that she was now the target. The moments slowed, her heartbeat thudding in an agonizingly slow rhythm in her ears. The gunman's glittering graphite eyes were fixed on her, and she put her hands up instinctively. She didn't take in much detail in that moment, only the piercing coldness of his eyes and the steadiness of that gun.

"Please don't—" Her mouth was moving, but she couldn't hear any words.

The slow motion in her mind suddenly caught up to real time as Mike took advantage of the gunman's distracted focus and sprinted forward. The man spun toward Mike at the same moment that Mike collided with him. A gunshot cracked through the air as they both landed on the ground. The gun skittered off under the car.

With a sob, Malory ran toward Katy on the porch, whose little mouth had formed the square shape of a terrified wail. Mike rammed a knee into the back of the man as he squirmed under Mike's weight.

"Hold on, big guy," Mike said gruffly. "Keep fighting me, and I'll only hurt you more, I can promise you that."

Malory gathered Katy up in her arms and sank to the grass next to her.

"Hey, babe," Mike said, grinning crookedly. "Thanks for the heads-up."

"Who is that?" she gasped.

"This?" Mike pulled out some cuffs and tightened them down onto the man's wrists until the smaller man winced. "He and I have a bit of a history. This is Sinclair Moody."

"Is he the one—?" She didn't finish, afraid to say too much.

"This is him." He patted the man on the back of the head. "Say, you were supposed to be in FBI custody, weren't you?" A car crunched into the driveway, and Mike nodded toward it. "Here they are now," he said with a grim smile.

"The thought of anything happening to you two—" Tears choked off her voice.

"Malory," he started, but the FBI agents were out of their car now and heading toward them—two big men in plain black suits who looked as though they meant business.

"Sheriff Cruise?" the first agent asked.

"Hold on—" Mike said testily and turned back to Malory. "I'm not asking you to stick around and see how it goes, Mal. I'm all in. I love you. I want you to be part of our family. I want to do this together."

"You've got to be kidding me!" Moody roared. "You're proposing with a knee in my back?"

"Shut up," Mike retorted, and rose to his feet, hauling the man up with him. "You're going with the feds. By the way, why isn't he in custody?" He cut the FBI agents a baleful look. "You told me he was in custody!"

"An embarrassing oversight," the FBI agent snapped. "It won't be repeated, I can assure you." He took Moody by one arm and angled him toward the car.

"Hey, that's my kid!" Moody shouted, jutting his chin toward Katy, who cowered in Malory's arms. "I've got legal rights to her!"

"No, that's where you're wrong," Mike barked back. "She's *my* kid. Enjoy prison!"

As Sinclair Moody was hauled off to the car, Mike sank down onto his knees and pulled Malory and Katy into his strong arms, holding them close against his chest. Malory closed her eyes, listening to the comforting thud of his heart.

"So what do you say?" he asked, his voice rumbling in his chest. "Will you marry me?"

Malory looked up into his face, stunned. A little hand tugged at her shirt.

"Nanny Mal?" Katy asked breathlessly. "Nanny Mal? Will you be my mommy?"

"Yes!" Malory pulled Katy into their embrace. "Yes, I'll marry you, Mike. And I'll be your new mommy, Katy."

Mike's arms tightened around them both and she closed her eyes, sinking into the love she felt. This was right—this was finally right. Her baby boy gave a little jump from within, and as she looked up, Mike's lips came down onto hers.

"Kisses!" Katy sang happily.

When Mike pulled back and her eyes fluttered open again, Malory found several more deputies and an FBI agent staring at them.

"Hello," she said weakly. The yard was now bustling with officers and another couple of squad cars were now arriving. Hope was like that—Hope took care of its own.

"Let's get you inside," Mike said, rising to his feet. He pulled her with him, then scooped her up into his arms. She let out a squeak and laughed as he carried her effortlessly toward the front door.

"Doctor's orders, remember?" He grinned. "Come on, Katy. Let's get Mommy inside."

Mommy. Malory liked the sound of that, and when

she would look back on this day, she would realize that this was exactly the kind of mother she wanted to be—the kind who protected her own and who loved her family with every ounce of strength she had.

* * * * *

MILLS & BOON®

Cherish™

EXPERIENCE THE ULTIMATE RUSH OF FALLING IN LOVE

A sneak peek at next month's titles...

In stores from 11th February 2016:

- **The Greek's Ready-Made Wife** – Jennifer Faye *and* **Fortune's Secret Husband** – Karen Rose Smith
- **Crown Prince's Chosen Bride** – Kandy Shepherd *and* **"I Do"...Take Two!** – Merline Lovelace

In stores from 25th February 2016:

- **Billionaire, Boss...Bridegroom?** – Kate Hardy *and* **A Baby and a Betrothal** – Michelle Major
- **Tempted by Her Tycoon Boss** – Jennie Adams *and* **From Dare to Due Date** – Christy Jeffries

---

Available at WHSmith, Tesco, Asda, Eason, Amazon and Apple

Just can't wait?
Buy our books online a month before they hit the shops!
visit www.millsandboon.co.uk

These books are also available in eBook format!

0216/23

MILLS & BOON®
The Sheikhs Collection!

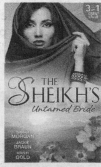
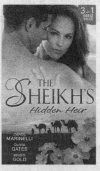

This fabulous 4 book collection features stories from some of our talented writers. The Sheikhs Collection features some of our most tantalising, exotic stories.

Order yours at
www.millsandboon.co.uk/sheikhscollection